PUFFIN BOOKS

Linda Chapman lives in Leicestershire with her husband, three children, two dogs and a pony. When she is not writing, she spends her time looking after her family, reading, talking to people about writing, and horse riding whenever she can.

You can find out more about Linda on her websites: *lindachapman.co.uk* and *lindachapmanauthor.co.uk*

Books by Linda Chapman

LINDA CHAPMAN

Loving Spirit Dreams

PUFFIN

PUFFIN BOOKS

Published by the Penguin Group
Penguin Books Ltd, 80 Strand, London WC2R 0RL, England
Penguin Group (USA) Inc., 375 Hudson Street, New York, New York 10014, USA
Penguin Group (Canada), 90 Eglinton Avenue East, Suite 700, Toronto, Ontario, Canada M4P 2Y3
(a division of Pearson Penguin Canada Inc.)
Penguin Ireland, 25 St Stephen's Green, Dublin 2, Ireland (a division of Penguin Books Ltd)
Penguin Group (Australia), 250 Camberwell Road, Camberwell, Victoria 3124, Australia
(a division of Pearson Australia Group Pty Ltd)
Penguin Books India Pvt Ltd, 11 Community Centre, Panchsheel Park, New Delhi – 110 017, India
Penguin Group (NZ), 67 Apollo Drive, Rosedale, North Shore 0632, New Zealand
(a division of Pearson New Zealand Ltd)
Penguin Books (South Africa) (Pty) Ltd, 24 Sturdee Avenue, Rosebank,
Johannesburg 2196, South Africa

Penguin Books Ltd, Registered Offices: 80 Strand, London WC2R 0RL, England

puffinbooks.com

First published 2011
1

Set in Sabon LT Std 12/16 pt
Typeset by Palimpsest Book Production Limited, Falkirk, Stirlingshire
Made and printed in Great Britain by Clays Ltd, St Ives plc

British Library Cataloguing in Publication Data
A CIP catalogue record for this book is available from the British Library

ISBN: 978-0-141-32833-1

www.greenpenguin.co.uk

To my parents for allowing me to have horses in my life and for all the love, support and encouragement they have always given me, whatever I am doing.

Listen and I will speak
Ask and I will answer

Spirit . . .

The stable was quiet. Outside, on the busy yard, life bustled by, but inside there was an air of peace and calm. The grey horse nuzzled Ellie's hands, his warm breath whispering across her fingers. *Oh, Spirit*, she thought, love swelling in her chest as she rested her head against his. They belonged to each other; they had done since the first time they'd met.

Ellie let her mind empty and lost herself in her horse's presence. Little by little she felt the energy that surrounded them starting to merge and their thoughts opening up to each other. The first few times Ellie had experienced this sensation of their minds connecting, she had been utterly astonished. She was more used to it now, but it still sent a thrill running through her. When it happened, she and Spirit were able to talk to each other, communicating with words, images and feelings.

Now, Spirit sent a picture of a hostile, unhappy black horse into her mind.

Lucifer, Ellie thought, with a flash of guilt.

He needs you. Spirit's words came to her.

Ellie knew she should be trying to help Lucifer, but she didn't want to, not after what the black horse had done. *I've tried talking to him. It's never worked*, she countered defensively.

You need to listen.

I do but he never talks to me.

No. Listen, Spirit repeated patiently.

Ellie mustered more arguments, but as usual he didn't push her. They moved on to speak about other things. Ten minutes passed and suddenly Spirit tensed. He lifted his head high and a single urgent word jumped straight into Ellie's head. *Go!*

Ellie blinked. *Go where?*

To Lucifer.

Lucifer? Fear gripped Ellie as she heard Spirit's alarm. *What's happening?*

He needs you now. Go!

As always, Ellie trusted Spirit absolutely. She didn't stop to ask more questions or to wonder how she felt about Lucifer. She turned and ran.

Three weeks earlier . . .

Chapter One

Ellie Carrington leant against the gate of the circular menage, a horse-training manual open in her hands, the breeze blowing through her long, wavy blonde hair. In the ring, a chestnut pony cantered round her cousin, Joe.

'He needs to go slower, I think!' Ellie called. 'It says here: "the horse should settle into a steady trot". Can you slow Solo down while keeping him going round the outside?'

'I think so.' Joe moved so he was level with the pony's neck. Solo instantly bounced to a stop. With a snort, he turned and raced in the other direction at an even faster canter than before.

Ellie giggled. 'Think again!'

Joe frowned in concentration, his greeny-grey eyes intent, his sandy-brown hair flopping over his forehead. His father's horse-showing yard – High Peak Stables – had a top-class reputation and Joe had ridden in the show ring all his life, but Ellie knew he was happiest like this, at home, working with a young horse. That morning, he was trying out a training technique called 'join-up'. It was a method based on understanding how horses acted in the wild, and using body language to communicate with them. It was particularly good for young horses and ponies like Solo when they were first being trained to wear a saddle and carry a rider.

Joe moved towards the pony's hindquarters, but that only made Solo go faster. He tried stepping closer to Solo's head, which made the pony stop, whizz round and change direction again. Joe stayed calm and patient, though. Finally, while staying level with the pony's stomach, he tried stepping back. It worked. Solo slowed to a trot.

Solo trotted round the ring several times, his movement gradually becoming rhythmical and relaxed. Whenever he slowed down too much, Joe moved towards his hindquarters, sending him on. After a few minutes, he began to experiment with making Solo change direction, using just eye contact and the positioning of his body. It was very peaceful in the early morning. The only sounds were the thud of Solo's hooves on the sand and his occasional snort ringing through the air. Behind the schooling ring rose the mountains of north Derbyshire, their peaks and ridges silhouetted against the pale blue sky. Sheep dotted the slopes, the black-faced ewes grazing, the lambs bouncing around.

'What should I look for next?' Joe called.

Ellie checked the book again. 'His ear should tilt towards you and he should start to lick and maybe chew. His head might lower even more.'

As she spoke, Solo's muzzle reached to the ground and he did exactly as she had just said. 'There! Look! That's him saying to you that he wants to join-up.'

Turning away from Solo, Joe dropped his gaze to the floor, lowering his head and rounding his shoulders. Solo slowed to a walk and then halted, looking at Joe's new non-threatening body position. Ellie had read that this was the crucial moment, the time when the pony would make the choice whether to come in and be close to the human in the middle, or decide to stay away. If he chose to come in, it would be his way of saying he trusted Joe and they could start backing him. If he chose to stay away, then Joe would turn back and continue to drive him on.

Solo hesitated and then walked towards the centre, stopping beside Joe's shoulder. *Yes!* Ellie thought, her breath leaving her in a rush. It had happened just like the book said it should!

Joe looked outwardly calm, but Ellie was sure he was just as delighted as she was – he didn't need the book to know what Solo coming in meant. After turning to gently rub the pony's face between his eyes, he walked away and Solo followed him. Wherever Joe went, so did the pony. He didn't *have* to be with the boy; he was choosing to be. By responding to the signals Solo had sent – the pony's way of saying in horse language that he wanted to be friends – Joe had shown Solo that he understood him. The first building blocks of trust had been laid.

'It's worked!' Joe said, coming to the gate.

He and Ellie smiled at each other, sharing the moment.

'Are you going to try putting the saddle on now?' Ellie asked.

Joe nodded.

Ellie had seen ponies being backed quite a few times and knew that usually they would buck and fight, scared of the weight of the saddle and the tightening of the girth round their stomachs. But as Joe put a headcollar on Solo, then took the saddle from the fence to place it on Solo's back, the pony stood quietly. As Joe fastened the girth, Solo tensed, but Joe reassured him, talking gently, and the pony relaxed again, trusting what Joe was doing.

When Joe asked him to walk on, the pony walked calmly beside him as if he'd had a saddle on his back every day of his life.

It was incredible to watch. Ellie remembered the last time she'd seen a pony being backed. It had been in New Zealand, before her parents had died. She'd been with her dad. They'd watched as the pony had thrown itself around.

'There has to be a better way,' her dad had said to her then.

Dad would have loved to see this, Ellie thought wistfully. *Mum too.*

Loss welled up painfully inside her. Last July, both her parents had died in a car crash. She could barely remember the time straight after, her grief had been completely overwhelming. But over the eight months since then, the intense pain had gradually faded. She still missed them every day, but most of the time now she could get by OK. Or at least she could until something like this happened – a moment that she would want to share with them – and then the fact that they were gone, that she would never see them again, would hit her full-on.

She had many tricks for dealing with the pain. Now, she focused on holding her breath, counting to ten and back again, waiting for the feelings to subside. She hoped Joe was too busy with Solo to notice. He would only ask what was wrong if he saw she was upset and she didn't like to talk about her mum and dad with anyone apart from Spirit.

As Ellie pictured Spirit's pricked ears and dark wise eyes, she felt as if the pain inside her was being wrapped in a blanket. Just the thought of Spirit could comfort her. It felt like he had been in her life forever, but it had only been two months since she had first seen him at a horse sale, bought him and led him back here to High Peak Stables. Back then the countryside had been gripped by winter, snow hugging the bare peaks, a bitter wind blowing across the yard every day, but now the air was warmer and yellow daffodils danced around the fence posts.

Ellie looked around. Even with spring softening the rugged bleakness of the mountains, the countryside here in the Peak District was far from the lush rolling hills of New Zealand where she had grown up. It still felt like a landscape that she didn't quite belong in – part of a life that wasn't really hers.

She had wanted to stay with her gran in New Zealand, but it had eventually been decided it was best for Ellie to move to England to live with her Uncle Len and sixteen-year-old cousin, Joe. Being only fourteen, she had no say in the matter. She wondered what her life would be like if she'd hadn't left New Zealand. It was hard to know how to feel about that, because then, of course, she wouldn't have met Joe or bought Spirit. Her mum had used to have a saying: '*every ending is another beginning*'. It was true, she realized. So many new things had begun since her life in New Zealand had ended . . .

Joe led Solo over to the gate, pulling her out of her thoughts. 'I'll make that do for today.'

Ellie tried to focus on the horse. 'He's being really

good. Why don't you try backing him?' In the book, it suggested you could back a horse in the first session with join-up.

'Not today.' Joe patted Solo. 'It would be daft to rush him.'

'But he looks really relaxed.' Ellie looked at him hopefully. 'I'll get on if you want.'

'Nope,' Joe said, starting to untack Solo. 'I'll leave it.'

'Go on!'

'No,' Joe didn't rise to her urging. 'He's not being ridden today.'

Ellie sighed. Joe's steady, thoughtful approach to life reminded her a lot of her dad who had been very patient and calm. She knew it was a good way to be with horses and she tried to be like that when she could, but it didn't come naturally. She was far more like her mum had been – a whirlwind who swept through life, hating to wait for anything, jumping into things head first. Still, at least they got things done, as her mum always used to say.

She took the saddle from Joe and they started to lead Solo in.

'I wonder what Dad would say if he could see what we'd just done.'

'Yeah.' Ellie couldn't wait to see her uncle's face when he saw them finally riding Solo. Her uncle was one of the top producers of show horses in the country, but he had no time for new techniques like join-up, preferring to stick with the traditional methods he'd known all his life. *They have to know who's boss*, he often said when talking about horses. He'd only agreed Joe could try and join-up with Solo because he thought handling was good for a young horse, but he'd made it clear he didn't think Joe would get far with saddling the pony.

'So, when are you going to show him what you've been doing?' Ellie asked curiously.

'I'm not.'

'What?' Ellie was taken aback. 'Why?'

Joe shrugged. 'I just don't see the point. You know Dad'll never come round to join-up himself and if I try and tell him how good it is, it'll only cause a massive row.'

'But if he sees you riding Solo and knows it's been done so easily, then he'll have to believe in it.'

Joe laughed drily. 'Is that a pig flying past me? Come on, Els, you know what Dad's like. He'll just say Solo's an easy pony and dismiss it that way and then we'll have an argument.'

'But if you're not going to show him what you've done, what's the point in doing it?' Ellie looked at him in frustration.

'The point is that it helps the horses.' Joe patted Solo affectionately. 'If I can get every youngster started like this, it'll make the whole process easier before Dad comes to them. That would be a good thing to do, wouldn't it?' he appealed.

'I guess,' Ellie agreed reluctantly. She still felt they should use the opportunity to show Uncle Len what could be achieved.

Joe saw her face. 'Ellie, you're not to say anything. It really would cause trouble. I don't want that.'

She looked at him.

'Promise you won't?'

She sighed. She could see why Joe didn't want to get into trouble with his dad. He had a fierce temper and often lashed out at Joe when he was angry. 'OK, I promise.'

They reached the pony barn. There were two American-style barns at High Peak Stables as well as two schooling rings and a smart main courtyard with neat hanging baskets, a wash barn, tackroom and rug-room, and ten spacious stables round three of the sides.

A small bay pony inside the barn whinnied shrilly as he heard their voices. He was too little to do more than poke his nose over the top of the door. Joe led Solo nearer and leant over to pat the pony's neck. 'Hey there, Merlin.'

Merlin had been Joe's first pony. He was kept on the yard for when children came for lessons with Len. 'He's looking well,' Ellie said, stroking Merlin over the door too. The pony nuzzled her hand, searching hopefully for treats.

'He's looking much *too* well with all this spring grass. He could do with some more exercise.'

'We could take him and Spirit out for a ride later,' Ellie suggested.

'My legs are down to his knees now!' Joe laughed.

'But you're not too heavy for him.' Although Joe was quite tall, he was slim and wiry. The sturdy Welsh pony would have no problem carrying his weight.

Joe didn't need much persuading; he still loved riding Merlin. 'OK. Should we go out at lunchtime?'

Ellie nodded. 'Cool!'

They smiled at each other and, as she met his familiar greeny-grey eyes, Ellie felt her heart skip a beat. In an instant, she was back to a time barely two weeks ago when she and Joe had almost kissed. They had been interrupted and neither of them had mentioned it since, but Ellie hadn't forgotten.

Her cheeks started to redden and she moved quickly away from the door, glad Joe couldn't read her mind. 'Shall . . . shall I put Solo away?'

Joe checked his watch. 'Look, it's almost seven o'clock. Dad'll be out for morning feeds in a few minutes. Why don't I sort Solo out, then you can see Spirit before feeding starts?'

'Thanks!' Ellie leapt gratefully at the thoughtful offer. Joe knew that once the morning routine started she would be too busy to see Spirit until lunchtime. 'I'll see you in the feedroom then.'

'Don't be late though, will you?' Joe said anxiously. 'You know it'll only make Dad cross.'

But Ellie was already hurrying away, her thoughts too full of seeing Spirit to reply.

Chapter Two

Spirit was kept in one of three large foaling stables set slightly away from the main courtyard down a quiet path. Len liked Spirit to be kept out of sight so that potential clients who came to look around the yard would not be put off by seeing him. Although Spirit was in much better condition than when Ellie had bought him at a horse sale, his ribs still showed and the scars on his legs and shoulder would be with him always.

'Spirit!' Ellie called softly as she turned down the path.

Spirit whickered, coming to his door. Slipping into the stable, Ellie could feel his happiness at seeing her. She would never forget the day they had first met. He had been standing in a metal pen, neglected and in very poor condition, but he'd lifted his head and stared straight at her and in that moment the world had changed; she'd felt like she knew him – that she had always known him. She'd never experienced anything like it in her life. The love had been instant and, once she had felt it, she had known she couldn't go home without him. Impulsively, she'd bought him and then had faced the task of persuading her uncle to let her keep him at High Peak Stables. It had been touch and go for a while, but eventually her uncle had agreed.

Stroking Spirit's neck, she slowed her breathing and focused. *Spirit?* she thought.

Several weeks into owning him, she had discovered that when she and Spirit were alone together, they could communicate with their minds. She didn't know how it happened, but if she relaxed and thought about nothing but him, their thoughts would connect and then she could ask him questions and he would reply. Ellie couldn't always understand exactly what he meant, but it was amazing to understand him even some of the time.

Ellie hadn't told anyone about being able to talk to Spirit. She'd once tried to tell Joe, but even he hadn't understood. She didn't blame him. She had to admit, it did sound incredibly weird. But it was true. They really could communicate.

Spirit? she thought again, concentrating her mind. She let the world shrink to just her and her horse, feeling the restless, burning energy that seemed to buzz through her most of the time begin to calm and settle. The air around her and Spirit seem to shift and then she felt the connection open.

Ellie.

Ellie felt a rush of delight. *Yes, I can hear you. Are you all right?*

Yes.

When they had first started talking, Spirit had shown her images of the neglect and harsh treatment he'd suffered at the trekking stables he had come from, the trauma he'd felt when he had been badly beaten in his earlier days at a showing home, and his early happy life as a foal. He had listened, too, as she'd shared her past with him – the pain-filled memories of her parents, things she hadn't wanted to talk about with anyone else. Now, although they still shared those things when they needed to, they also had a simpler daily communication as well.

Into her head came a picture of the field behind the stables.

You'd like to go out in the field? she guessed.

A wave of positive energy flooded towards her. *Yes.*

Ellie saw a new picture, this time of herself riding Spirit. *And you'd like to be ridden?*

Only by you.

I'll ride you later, Ellie told him. *We'll go out in the woods with Joe and Merlin later.*

She became aware of a slight ache in her bones, particularly lower down her legs. She frowned, wondering if the feeling was coming from Spirit, but as soon as she started to focus on it, it disappeared.

She waited to see if she felt it again but she didn't.

A picture of the field pushed back into her mind, this time with Spirit grazing in it in the spring sun.

Ellie smiled. *OK, I get the message. You can go out straight after breakfast.* She realized time must be passing and, stepping back, she let the connection between them fade.

As she did so, she heard doors banging on the yard and horses whinnying. She glanced at her watch. It was ten past seven. She'd lost track of time. 'Oh, great,' she groaned under her breath, suddenly remembering Joe's warning about not being late for morning feeds. 'I must go,' she told Spirit. 'I'll be back with your breakfast soon.'

Shutting his door, Ellie hurried back towards the main yard. Even though she knew she was late, she was buzzing inside. She loved talking to Spirit. In the last few weeks, she'd also been wondering if she could talk to other horses in the same way. Picasso, one of the ponies she rode for her uncle, had become scared of the horsebox and so she'd tried to speak to him. She hadn't managed to communicate with him as she did with Spirit, but she'd felt a slight connection and was sure he'd understood what she was saying even if he hadn't replied. Afterwards he seemed to trust her more and, with Spirit's calming presence, she'd managed to get him into the horsebox. She'd attempted to talk to him a few more times since then, but so far he still hadn't actually answered. She kept hoping that one day he would – it would be amazing to speak properly with other horses too.

Maybe if I just keep trying, she thought hopefully.

Reaching the feedroom, she found Uncle Len mixing the feeds while Joe piled up the buckets ready to take them to the pony barn. The yard was busy now. The grooms – Stuart, Helen and Sasha – had arrived and were busy refilling water buckets, and Luke, Joe's eighteen-year-old cousin from the other side of the family who worked full time for Len, was on his way to the hay barn to get the haynets.

Len looked up with a frown as Ellie came into the feedroom. He was a short stocky man with grey hair cropped close to his head. His eyes were the same grey-blue as Ellie's, but far harder, like granite. 'You're late.'

Ellie felt her temper prickle, but she controlled it. If she wanted to keep Spirit on the yard, she had to keep on the right side of her uncle. She couldn't risk making him angry even though she hated his bullying ways. She gritted her teeth but kept her voice level. 'I'm sorry. I was just with Spirit. I lost track of time.'

Her uncle's expression left her in no doubt that he didn't think that a good excuse. 'If that horse of yours is going to start interfering with your work . . .' The threat was left hanging in the air.

'He's not,' Ellie said quickly.

'We did some good work with Solo this morning, Dad,' Joe broke in, trying to deflect attention from Ellie. 'He joined-up and everything.'

His distraction worked. Len snorted. 'Joined-up!' He pointed the mixing stick at Joe. 'You'd be far better concentrating on the show ring, not messing about with daft things like "joining-up".'

Joe didn't reply. He simply bent his head and started to pile up buckets. Len watched him and blew out a scornful breath through his teeth. 'Don't you go getting ideas about things like that. It's the show ring that matters. Just you remember that.'

Ellie felt herself really struggling not to say something as Joe responded with a nod, keeping the peace as best he could. 'Should Ellie and I go and give these out, Dad?'

Len grunted. 'Yes and no hanging about. We've got a busy morning. First off, I want the two of you in the ring on Barney and Picasso – they need some jumping practice. Troy needs to be brushed over and tacked up, as well. I'll ride him straight after you've schooled those ponies; he was messing about yesterday. Right –' he mixed the last feed up and thrust it at them – 'get yourselves moving.'

Ellie and Joe headed out on to the yard.

'I don't know how you put up with your dad sometimes!' Ellie muttered under her breath as she finally let out her anger. 'He thinks he rules the world!'

'I guess he does rule this little bit of it here on the yard.' Joe caught her eye. 'There's no point getting wound up about it, Els. Just let it go.'

'How do you do that, though?' Ellie appealed.

Joe smiled drily. 'Practice.'

As they walked past the end stable of the courtyard, a black horse flew at the door. They stopped and watched him toss his head angrily. It was a new show horse called Lucifer. He'd arrived the evening before. He was jet-black with just a small white star, but ever since he'd come he'd been squealing at the other horses and threatening to bite anyone who went near his stable.

'He's not settled in yet, has he?' said Joe.

Ellie shook her head. 'He's beautiful though. Do you think he'll do well in the ring?'

'He'd better. Or there's going to be trouble with Jeff Hallett.'

Lucifer was owned by Jeff Hallett whose company, Equi-Glow, sponsored High Peak Stables. Equi-Glow was a horse-food manufacturer and the sponsorship was worth a lot of money because it provided the yard with free feed. It was really important that Lucifer was successful.

'So how's it going to work?' Ellie asked curiously. 'Is Mr Hallett going to ride Lucifer himself?'

'No. He's for Anna, Jeff's daughter. She wants to go in the hack classes, but she's at uni now and so Dad will produce him and train him, and for the shows Anna can't make, Dad'll take him in.'

'He's wild,' said Ellie, looking at the black gelding who was now weaving from side to side, radiating hostility.

Joe nodded and glanced around. 'Come on. He'll settle down soon. We'd best not hang about.'

They went to the barn and emptied the feeds into the ponies' mangers. Then leaving Joe to wash out the buckets, Ellie headed to the hay store to fetch the ponies' haynets. Luke was in there with his terrier dog, Pip. Tall and dark-haired, Luke had come to live and work on the yard a year and a half ago when he had left his expensive boarding school. Ellie didn't know much about Luke's family life, but Joe had told her that his parents were rich, he hadn't had the happiest of childhoods and he had spent many of his school holidays at High Peak Stables with Joe and his dad.

'Morning,' he greeted Ellie.

'Hi,' she said. Luke was the complete opposite of Joe – swaggering, confident, and seemed to be only interested in shows and chatting up girls. To start with he had really irritated Ellie, but at her first show a few weeks ago he'd given her some good advice and helped her get Picasso ready. He'd seemed in his element there – completely focused on the horses and loving the atmosphere. Ellie had had a brilliant time too, and since then she'd begun to feel there was more to Luke than the brazen act he put on.

'So what were you and Joe doing out on the yard so early?' he asked curiously as she began to help him sort the haynets into piles, while Pip hunted for mice among the stacked-up bales of hay. 'I saw you bringing Solo in.'

She nodded. 'Joe had just been joining-up with him.'

Luke's eyes glinted with humour. 'Oh, I see – *horse-whispering*.'

Ellie felt a flash of irritation. 'Don't just dismiss something when you know nothing about it! You're as bad as Uncle Len.'

'Me? Never,' Luke protested. 'I just don't see why you want to mess about with things like that. Len's ways work. He's won enough in the ring.'

Ellie bristled. 'It's not just about winning!'

Luke raised his eyebrows. 'Isn't it?'

'No!'

He gave her an amused look. 'Say what you like, Ellie, but you like to win too. I know you do. I saw it at that last show we went to. And you know there's no point doing stuff like join-up here. You'll never convince Len to use horse-whispering ways. I mean, can you imagine him chatting to a horse before it went into the ring – what's he going to say? "Come on, Picasso, I'll give you a carrot if you do a great gallop?"'

'See, you don't know anything about it!' Ellie said hotly. 'Horse-whispering isn't about actually *whispering* to horses. It's about listening to them, reading their body language and –'

She broke off as she saw Luke's broad grin. 'Gotcha!'

Ellie let out an exclamation of annoyance. Of course Luke knew perfectly well what horse-whispering was about even if he chose not to try it. He had just been winding her up, refusing to take things seriously as always. 'Oh, you . . .' She swung round crossly to pick up three haynets to take to the ponies. As she did so, she caught her foot in a long piece of bale string. She would have gone flying if Luke hadn't stepped forward and grabbed her just in time. He steadied her.

'Have a good trip?' he enquired.

Ellie flushed and pulled her arm away, embarrassed. Just then, a pretty girl with straightened blonde hair and lashings of dark eyeliner came in. It was Sasha, the junior groom on the yard, and Luke's girlfriend for the last four weeks.

'There you are,' she said to Luke. 'Didn't you hear me calling you?'

'Sorry, babe. I was just . . .' Luke glanced at Ellie and grinned. 'Just helping Ellie out.'

Sasha immediately gave Ellie a suspicious, narrow-eyed look.

Oh, pur–lease! Ellie thought, almost laughing out loud at the thought she would be anything like Sasha and fawn all over Luke for his attention.

'I'm taking these to the ponies.' Ignoring the older girl's death-ray stare, she grabbed as many haynets as she could carry.

'Watch your step, Ellie!' Luke called innocently as she left the hay store.

Ellie had to bite back her laugh. She wouldn't give him the satisfaction of knowing he'd made her smile – his ego wouldn't be able to cope! Shaking her head, she carried the haynets down the yard.

Chapter Three

The morning passed in a bustle of activity as the horses were groomed and exercised, and the stables mucked out. As well as Luke, the three grooms worked full-time on the yard: Stuart, an ex-jockey in his forties, was the yard manager; Helen, his girl-friend, was the senior groom; and Sasha was the junior groom. Ellie and Joe helped whenever they weren't at school. The Easter holidays had just started, so Ellie knew they could expect to be on the yard from dawn until dusk, often longer.

Len's standards were exacting. He never failed to let anyone know if a horse they brought out to be ridden was in a state below his expectations. The yard was swept twice a day, tack cleaned every time it was used, stables bedded down with thick beds of clean straw or shavings, and the feed and water buck-ets always scrubbed. Anyone who cut corners or was caught not working would be shouted or even sworn at. Len was tireless himself and he wouldn't tolerate laziness or slackness.

Despite her uncle's brusqueness and temper, Ellie enjoyed working on such a professional yard. It was hard work but exciting, and the horses were amazing to ride. Len had made no secret of the fact he hoped for a stellar year from his show team. Ellie would ride the smaller ponies and Joe the larger ponies, while Luke rode the Intermediates and riding horses and Len the hunters and hacks. As well as Len's own horses and ponies, there were the liveries he produced for clients and took to shows. The aim was to get as many horses and ponies as possible qualified for the two big shows in the season – the Royal International Horse Show at Hickstead in July, and the Horse of the Year show in October which everyone called HOYS. Everything was focused towards that – and to winning once they got there.

'Do you still want to go out for a ride at lunchtime?' Joe asked Ellie as they fetched brooms to sweep the yard later that morning.

'Definitely.' It was a lovely day and Ellie was really looking forward to just ambling along on Spirit, chatting to Joe. Spirit and Merlin were great friends too. She knew they'd like to be out together.

She and Joe went to the muck heap and began sweeping up the loose straw. Helen and Sasha were riding out on Hereward and Oscar, two of the hunters, and Stuart was lunging Milly, one of the ponies Ellie rode, in the circular ring. Luke was in the main schooling ring nearby, helping Len with Troy, a young working hunter, who was refusing to jump.

Ellie watched while she swept. Troy was a gentle giant of a horse and usually very willing to please, but today he had his ears back. Every time Len turned him towards a jump he stopped dead and ran backwards, despite Len swearing at him and digging in his spurs.

Ellie frowned. Troy's bay coat was dark with sweat. 'There's something wrong with him,' she said suddenly.

'What do you mean?' Joe asked, stopping sweeping to look at the horse.

Ellie couldn't explain it, but it was as if she could feel the pain pulsing off Troy. She'd always been able to sense animals' emotions and feelings, and since she'd started talking to Spirit that ability had grown stronger. 'He's in pain.' She saw Joe give her a strange look. 'I imagine,' she added hastily. 'Dad always said that horses usually only play up if they're hurting or scared.'

Joe nodded thoughtfully. 'My books say that too.'

Luke picked up a long lunge whip and cracked it behind the horse's back legs. Even though Ellie knew Luke had just cracked the whip in the air and it hadn't touched the horse, she still flinched. Troy leapt forward at the sharp sound.

'Get him across the back legs as I come up to the fence this time!' Len ordered.

Ellie couldn't bear it. Troy was in pain. She could feel it. They shouldn't be hitting him to force him to jump. She started forward impulsively. 'No!'

'Ellie!' Joe grabbed her arm in alarm. 'What are you doing?'

She struggled against him wildly. 'They mustn't hit him! There's something wrong!'

'You don't know that for sure. Anyway, Dad's not going to stop just because you say!' Joe saw her face. 'Think of Spirit, Els. If you make Dad really mad, he might say you can't keep him here any more. Then what will you do? There's nowhere close enough you could cycle or walk to. You've got to be sensible!'

Every bone in Ellie's body wanted to stop what was happening in the ring, but she knew what Joe was saying was right. Whether she liked it or not, her uncle had a hold on her. She looked back at the ring, completely torn.

'I hate it too,' Joe told her more quietly, still holding her arm. 'You know I do, but we can't do anything about it. We just can't.'

Troy was slowing down as he approached the jump. 'Now!' Len's angry voice allowed no argument. 'Get him!'

Luke caught the bay across the back legs with the cord of the whip. Troy leapt forward and this time jumped. He cleared the fences and came round again. His eyes rolled fearfully as he saw Luke with the whip but he jumped without hesitation.

When he had jumped the fences three times, Len brought the horse back to a trot. He patted Troy's neck. 'Well, we got there in the end. Stubborn sod.' He let the horse walk round on a loose rein to cool off.

Luke came in from the menage. Ellie glared at him as he passed.

'What?' he said, seeing her look.

'You shouldn't have hit Troy like that,' she said accusingly.

Luke frowned. 'It worked.'

'But you didn't stop to think why he wasn't jumping. There might be something wrong with him!'

'Len checked though. He's not lame, his mouth's fine. There was no reason for him to be acting up like that.'

But Ellie wasn't appeased. She knew what she'd felt when she'd looked at Troy. 'There *is* something wrong. I'm just sure there is. I bet you didn't look hard enough.'

Luke rolled his eyes. 'Give me strength. I suppose you'd have had a little chat with him and then it would all have been OK?'

'Don't be stupid!' Ellie glared at him, not in the mood for joking now.

'Ellie,' Joe put in. 'Luke didn't have a choice. He

was only doing what Dad said. He couldn't have done anything else.'

Ellie turned on him angrily. 'You said you thought there was something wrong with Troy too and you certainly don't believe that's how horses should be treated. Don't take his side!'

'It's not about taking sides,' Joe protested. 'I'm just saying Luke had to do what Dad told him.'

Ellie looked from one to the other and then, with an angry exclamation, she walked away.

'Hormones,' she heard Luke say knowingly to Joe.

It took all her self-control not to go back and slap him. She reached the courtyard and then took a breath. What should she do? Really she should carry on sweeping but she wasn't going back to the muck heap while Luke was still there. Instead she went to the field and brought Spirit in.

He saw her opening the gate and came trotting over, ears pricked. As he reached her, Ellie felt a rush of relief. Being with Spirit always made her feel calmer. She stroked his ears and cheekbones, letting her upset over the argument with Luke fade away.

'I don't know what I'd do without you,' she whispered to him. 'You're more important than anything. I love you so much, Spirit.'

Spirit lifted his muzzle to her face. She smiled. She didn't need their minds to be connected to know that he was saying it back.

Buckling on Spirit's headcollar, she took him back to his stable. Her thoughts turned to Luke and Joe. Time after time, when she was irritated with Luke, Joe would step in and defend him. She shook her head. Joe was too nice at times. By rights, he should thoroughly dislike Luke. After all, his dad had never made any secret of the fact that he wished Joe was more like Luke. Joe had been small for ages and slightly built, no good at sports and far quieter than Len. Not at all competitive, he would never willingly have gone in shows, but it had turned out he was very successful in the ring and won a lot. He was a brilliant and gentle rider and the more sensitive horses really responded to him. And despite having so many reasons to dislike Luke, Joe didn't. They weren't best friends or anything but they always got on just fine.

Ellie put Spirit in his stable and went back on the yard. Joe was just coming down from the muck heap with the two brooms. 'It's all done up there. You OK?' he asked.

She nodded, not wanting to talk about it. 'Thanks for doing the sweeping. Do you still want to go out for a ride?'

'Definitely. Though I can't stay out for long. Helen's just asked me if I can help her this lunchtime. She wants to leave an hour early today, so she's going to work through her lunch break and she needs someone to hold Pericles and Hereward while she trims them. There's no one else around – Stu's with Dad planning the show schedule, and Luke and Sasha are having lunch together. So is it OK if we just have a quick ride? It'll be difficult for Helen to do the horses on her own.'

'Sure.' Ellie said. It was typical of Joe to cut his lunch break short to help someone out.

They headed out as soon as they could, riding into the woods that clustered on the slopes behind the stables.

Spirit and Merlin walked side by side, ears pricked. Although Merlin was almost twenty, he was very sprightly. He was a sweet-natured pony, always eager to please.

'How many years have you had Merlin?' Ellie asked curiously.

'Ten. I got him when I was six,' Joe replied. 'I was just coming out of the lead-rein classes. I'd had a mad little pony called Pepper – he was good on the lead rein but a nutter off.'

'I didn't know you'd done lead-rein classes.' Ellie giggled. She had seen the lead-rein ponies at the show she'd been to. Their riders had looked very cute in their tiny polished jodhpur boots and the large velvet hats that made their heads look too large for their bodies. The girls had all worn red ribbons in their hair. She looked at Joe teasingly. 'Bet you looked lovely in red hair ribbons.'

'Ha ha.' Joe grinned. 'I looked very smart in my show outfit I'll have you know.'

'Did your dad used to lead you?' Ellie couldn't imagine it.

'No, Mum did.' Joe rarely talked about his mum. She and Len had divorced when Joe was eight and she lived in Devon now. It was a long drive so Joe only visited occasionally. Ellie had seen pictures of her in Joe's room. She had the same sandy-brown hair as him and a wide, friendly smile. It was hard to imagine her being married to Len. But then Ellie found it hard to imagine anyone being married to her uncle.

Joe changed the subject back to the pony. 'Anyway, I got Merlin when I was six. He always looked after me in the show ring. I swear he used to watch the other ponies jump the course and then he'd simply take me round. He's brilliant, aren't you, boy? Best pony ever.'

Merlin tossed his head as if aware he was being praised.

They rode on for a few minutes in a companionable silence. Ellie thought back to that morning. She'd loved watching Joe work with Solo. He was so good at things like that – so patient and keen to try things out. She glanced at him curiously.

'Do you still think about working on a different yard when you leave school?' Joe was due to leave in a few months after his GCSEs and he had once told her he would love to work on a yard specializing in natural horsemanship, a yard that helped problem horses. Ellie's stomach clenched. She hated the thought of him leaving but if it was what he really wanted, then maybe he should do it . . .

'I'd love to,' Joe replied. 'But Dad would never agree to it. He expects me to work here.'

Ellie shrugged. 'So?'

Joe smiled at her reaction. 'So . . . I just know I couldn't enjoy myself if I felt I'd let him down. Anyway, it's OK here. Well, it has been since you arrived . . .' He stopped himself.

Ellie looked up, surprised. She could see a hint of pink on his cheekbones.

'Should we . . . should we jump some logs?' Joe said hastily. 'There's a whole load of them through the trees over there.'

Not waiting for her reply, he turned down a narrow path and trotted on. Spirit pulled after Merlin and Ellie let him follow. Her thoughts were suddenly whirling. Joe liked her. She'd seen him blush just now! She'd thought he had forgotten that moment in the horsebox a couple of weeks ago when they'd almost kissed. But now she wondered, had he been thinking about it too?

Ellie's heart flipped in her chest at the idea that, maybe, they could be more than just friends. Joe was so kind and thoughtful. Cute too. They liked the same things, got on so well. It would be perfect!

But no. Not perfect, she quickly realized. There would be problems. He was her cousin and they lived in the same house. Her uncle would definitely freak at the idea. Still . . . could they keep it secret?

'Here we go!' Joe slowed Merlin down and pointed ahead to some fallen logs scattered across a clearing. 'Shall I go first?'

Ellie nodded, trying to sound normal. She wanted time to think about everything. 'I've never jumped Spirit before.'

'Do you want to or would you rather leave it?'

'No, no, I'll try it.'

Joe grinned. 'I'd have been really surprised if you'd said you were going to leave it!' He cantered over the first log on Merlin.

Spirit pulled at the bit and Ellie gave him his head. They approached the log and Spirit flew over it. She grinned as they landed.

'Brilliant!' called Joe.

Spirit was already tossing his head as he looked at the next log.

'Come on then, Spirit!' Ellie said. He plunged forward, and everything else vanished from her mind as she laughed and lost herself in the swift beat of his hooves.

Chapter Four

When they returned to the yard, Troy was looking out of his stable. Keeping well out of the reach of Lucifer next door, Ellie went over.

'Hey there, fella.'

The bay nuzzled at her hands in a friendly way. He was a loving horse, always seeking out fuss and company. 'Why didn't you jump today, Troy?' she murmured, stroking him. 'It's not like you. Is something the matter?'

Troy stared at her. Ellie wished she could talk to him like she did to Spirit and find out if there really was something wrong.

Why not?

She thought about it. She'd been meaning to talk to other horses. There was no harm in trying with Troy, was there? Opening the stable door, she slipped inside.

Troy pushed at her with his nose. Ellie wondered what to do now. When she was with Spirit she simply shut her eyes and they would connect, but Spirit was her horse – her special horse. There'd always been a bond between them. She hesitated and waited for an answer to come to her.

Just let him know you care, she thought.

Stroking his neck, she let the feelings of love that she felt for every horse build inside her and then sent them out to him.

Troy? What's wrong? You can talk to me.

Nothing happened.

I just want to help you, she said in her mind. Still nothing changed.

Ellie felt a prickle of impatience but made herself breathe calmly. Stroking his face and neck, she focused on sending him even more love. The air around them seemed to shift slightly. *It's working!* Ellie thought, recognizing the feeling. *Oh wow!*

Almost instantly the connection faded.

She quickly focused back on him, pushing her emotions down. *It's OK. I'm listening. Can you hear me still, Troy?*

Yes.

He'd replied! Distracted, she managed to stop herself being carried away and forced herself to concentrate.

What's wrong, Troy? Why didn't you want to jump today?

A grainy picture came into her mind. It was blurry

at first and she couldn't make it out, but gradually she began to see that it was a saddle. Feeling a stabbing pain across her shoulders, she flinched. *What do you mean?* she asked. *What are you trying to tell me?*

The pain came again.

Is it your saddle that's hurting you?

Yes.

Why?

Another image – this time of Troy a few months ago when he had just been brought back into work after his winter rest – filled her mind. He was skinnier, less muscular, she could see. In the last two months, with solid feed and daily exercise, his muscles had filled out, his back had broadened and his neck thickened. But why was he showing her this?

She hazarded a guess. *Are you trying to tell me the saddle used to fit you but it doesn't any more?*

Yes.

So that's why you refused today?

He blew on her hands. *Yes*, he repeated. He looked at her, eyes full of hope that she could help.

Ellie stroked him. So there *was* a problem. She'd been right. But more importantly it was a problem that could be cured. *Don't worry*, she told the big hunter. *I'll sort it out. I'll make it better.* Determination swept through her. *You're going to be OK.*

*

Thinking hard about what to do, Ellie left the stable. She was sure her uncle would just dismiss it if she told him she knew Troy's saddle was hurting him. Stuart however, tended to listen more. She waited until the yard manager came out of the farmhouse and then went over.

'Stuart? I've been thinking about Troy. You know he was refusing today?'

Stuart paused and nodded.

'Well, when I was in New Zealand,' she invented, 'Mum had a horse who started refusing. It turned out his saddle wasn't fitting him properly. He had put on some weight and the saddle was pinching him. Could it be the same thing with Troy maybe?'

Stuart considered it. 'Perhaps. He's certainly muscled-up well these last two months. Tell you what, why don't you get his saddle and I'll take a look at it?'

Ellie fetched Troy's saddle and met Stuart at the stable. As soon as Troy saw the saddle he backed away. He gave Ellie a look.

'It's OK,' she soothed him. 'We're going to sort this out.' She wasn't sure if he could understand her without them being connected, but her voice seemed to settle him and he stood still.

Stuart unbuckled Troy's rug and the bay threw his head up apprehensively. A frown creased Stuart's brow. 'Well, he's not looking too happy, I'll give you that.'

He placed the saddle carefully on Troy's back and fastened the girth. As the saddle was pulled snugly into place, Troy swished his tail. Stuart started feeling around the front of the saddle, seeing how it fitted against Troy's withers and shoulders. 'It *is* pinching him,' he said, glancing at Ellie in surprise. 'You're right. Poor lad.' He patted Troy's neck and unfastened the girth, then heaved off the saddle and ran a hand lightly over the horse's back. Troy flinched. 'He must be bruised. We'll get the saddler to sort this out and give Troy a few days off, then hopefully he'll be back to his usual self. Well done for figuring it out.'

Ellie grinned at him. 'Thanks!'

While Stuart went to tell Len, Ellie raced to the field to tell Spirit what had happened. He was grazing by the fence. When he heard her calling him, he lifted his head and trotted over. Ellie was buzzing with excitement. She checked no one was near and tried to calm herself enough to talk to him. At first nothing happened, but as she breathed in and out slowly, the connection between them opened.

She told him all about speaking with Troy. *Does it mean I can talk with any horse, Spirit?*

Yes

Ellie caught her breath, thinking about the possibilities. The different horses she knew ran through her head: Picasso, Gem, Milly, Merlin . . . What would they say to her? It would be amazing! Pictures of a future where she talked to any horse she wanted to filled her mind.

A new feeling of caution came from Spirit.

She looked at him, wondering what he meant.

Try and listen. Don't rush. Be patient.

She nodded. *I will. Of course I will.*

Trying to calm her excitement, she rested her head against his neck. As she did so, she became aware that something didn't feel quite right about him. She focused on the sensation and began to feel a slight ache in her bones, particularly lower down her legs. It was exactly the same feeling she'd had that morning.

She wondered if the feelings came from him. To check, she sent the sensation of pain gently back. *Spirit, are you feeling like this?*

Yes, he replied.

Ellie felt worried. *Is it because of the jumping? Did we do too much today?*

No. It's just how I feel sometimes.

What can I do?

Nothing. I'll be fine. Spirit sent her waves of reassurance.

She stroked him. *Are you sure?*

Yes, he answered.

Smoothing down his mane, she tried to trust him and not to worry.

*

'That was good thinking about Troy today, lass,' Len said that evening. He was putting a tray of chips into the oven, while Ellie and Joe were setting the table and Luke was getting a ham out of the fridge to carve. The kitchen had a quarry-tiled floor and piles of magazines on the surfaces. 'Very good thinking indeed.'

Ellie glowed, not because her uncle was pleased – that didn't really matter to her – but because it looked as if Troy would get better now. The saddler had been that afternoon and confirmed Troy's saddle was pinching behind his withers, making it painful to jump. The saddle had been taken away for adjusting and Troy could rest until he was better. Ellie was so pleased she'd been able to help.

The phone rang and Len answered it, taking it through into the lounge.

'What made you think it might be Troy's saddle?' Joe asked her curiously.

'I just remembered it had happened to a horse Mum once had,' Ellie said. She looked at Luke who was putting the ham on the table. Pip had jumped on a chair and was looking hopefully at the meat. Luke pulled off a bit of the fat and fed it to her, then sat down, and she jumped on to his knee. Ellie still felt cross with him from earlier. 'I told you there was something wrong with Troy,' she said.

'OK.' Luke held up his hands from stroking Pip.

'Guilty as charged. You were right. I was wrong. I'll listen next time.'

Ellie's eyes narrowed suspiciously. Was he laughing at her? But for once he didn't seem to be.

Len came back in. 'That was Jeff Hallett on the phone. He's coming to see that new horse of his tomorrow – bringing Anna too.'

'So what's she like – Anna Hallett?' Luke asked curiously.

'Don't even go there.' Len fixed him with a look, half good-humoured, half warning. 'The Equi-Glow deal's too important to have you mucking it up by breaking Jeff's daughter's heart.'

Luke raised his hands innocently. 'Len, I don't know *what* you mean.'

Len chuckled. 'Just you leave Anna Hallett alone, lad. As for the horse, what do you think of him then?'

'Lucifer's a stunner,' said Luke. 'A devil in the stable, though.'

'He'll calm down when he's been here a day or two. He's just been spoilt rotten at his old home,' Len shrugged. 'His owner only had him and he'd been with her since he was a youngster. She's been too soft with him. He's dominant,' he pronounced. 'It's written all over him. Wants to be the boss. But that isn't a bad thing in a show horse. Hereward's the same, and Starlight too. When they go in the ring they look as if they own it. If this one wins half as much as them, then I'll be a very happy man. And so will Jeff Hallett. What that daughter of his wants she gets, so if she wants to ride in the hack class at HOYS nothing else will do. We have to qualify him or else . . .' He shot a quick look at Joe before turning back to Luke. 'What would you say if I offered you the ride on him?'

Luke sat up instantly. 'Me? Ride him in the small hack classes? Definitely!'

Len looked at him assessingly. 'You're young to ride professionally in the hacks, but there's no denying you've got the killer instinct in the ring. It's daft holding you back. I reckon you'll do a grand job. If you don't, then you lose the ride and I'll take over. I can't afford any cock-ups with this horse.'

'I won't let you down, Len,' Luke vowed. Pip sensed his excitement and leapt up to lick his chin.

Len's eyes swept back to Joe. 'What do you think about that then?' There was an unmistakable challenge in his voice. 'Wish it were you riding it, do you?'

'No,' Joe shrugged. 'It's great, Dad. Luke'll do a good job on Lucifer.'

Len's face darkened. Instantly Ellie knew he had wanted Joe to care more – to be more like him and Luke.

'It'll be a long time before you get in the horse ring if Luke does well with that hack,' he said warningly.

'He'll get the rides on the hacks and hunters before you.'

'Yeah.' Joe nodded. 'But that's fine by me.' He picked up a magazine from the table.

There was a moment's pause while Len looked at him. Ellie could almost feel the tension building inside her uncle. Suddenly it exploded. 'You flamin' waste of space! Do you know how hard I worked to get this – all of it? It's so damned easy for you, isn't it?' He stabbed his finger towards Luke. 'Luke understands. He's got what it takes. Even she's got it,' he said, pointing at Ellie. 'Not like you,' he said, turning back to Joe. 'You useless piece of –' He broke off with a string of swear words and strode out, shaking his head.

There was a long silence. Joe's face burnt red. Ellie felt rooted to the spot. She saw Luke look at Joe, raising his eyebrows as if to ask if he was OK. Joe nodded and stood up, heading upstairs.

Ellie went after him. 'Joe? Are you all right?'

'Yeah.' He went into his bedroom on the first floor. She followed him, shutting the door behind them.

Joe saw her anxious face. 'Don't worry, Ellie. You know I'm used to it. Dad hates the fact I'm not more like him. He's told me that my whole life.'

Ellie's heart went out to him. Her parents might not be here any more, but neither of them would ever have spoken to her the way Len had to Joe. She couldn't imagine what it must be like to grow up with a father who always made you feel useless. 'He shouldn't say those things!' she said fiercely. 'No dad should.'

'That's the way he is.' Joe shrugged.

Impulsively, she went over and touched his arm. They looked at each other and, for an instant, Ellie was taken back to their hack in the woods earlier that day, remembering what she had been thinking then. Should she say something?

But Joe stepped back and the moment had gone. 'I should get changed for supper.'

He started to move around the room, picking up clothes.

Ellie's breath left her. 'Me too,' she said, stepping back towards the door. 'I'll see you downstairs in a bit.'

Leaving his room, she headed up the staircase to her bedroom, her thoughts jumping around in her head. She'd been within a split second of mentioning the moment in the horsebox. Her stomach curled at the thought. What would he have said?

She knew it hadn't been the right time for that. Joe was upset. But she couldn't help wondering what he felt about her. Reaching the landing, she stopped and looked back – was he thinking about her too?

The evening meal that night was a very quiet one. Afterwards, Joe disappeared to do some revision and, not wanting to watch football with her uncle and Luke, Ellie went to read in her bedroom. It was an old-fashioned room up on the second floor with a dark wooden wardrobe, a bed and chest of drawers. Since moving in, she'd bought a brightly striped rug and a new white duvet cover with a red and blue border, and put some photos in frames, but if anything the new things just made the old furniture look even more gloomy in contrast.

Sitting down on the bed, she picked up one of Joe's books about training horses from her bedside table and began to read. This book wasn't about join-up, but taught that you could build up a relationship with a horse by doing a lot of work, leading the horse from the ground and massaging it. She found it fascinating to read about so many training techniques – they all used different methods but most of them were founded on the same principle of forming a relationship with a horse based on trust and understanding.

Though I can do that anyway, she thought, looking at a black-and-white photo in the book of a woman leading a pony over a grid of poles. *I don't need to do these things. I can just talk to horses.*

Ellie hugged herself in delight as she remembered how she had talked to Troy that day. She couldn't believe how lucky she was. A mad dream of the future leapt into her head. Maybe, she and Joe could have a yard together. They could work with youngsters and troubled horses, he could use the horse-whispering techniques from the books and she could actually talk to them, link her mind with theirs to find out what was troubling or upsetting them. Between them, they would be able to help so many horses. *And we could go in shows too*, Ellie thought. *Or at least I could.*

The dream rapidly expanded as she saw them buying problem horses, making them better and then winning lots of shows with them before selling them on to good homes, so they could buy more horses and do it all over again . . .

Spirit would be with her too, of course; he would always be with her until he died. She picked up a hairbrush from the bedside table. It was a future she liked. Pulling the brush through her tangled hair, she smiled.

Chapter Five

'There's a good boy,' Joe soothed, while Ellie walked round Solo the next morning, putting weight on the stirrups with her hands, stroking over his body, checking the girth, adjusting the bridle and moving the bit around in Solo's mouth. It had only taken a short time before Solo had joined-up with Joe that morning. He stood happily as Joe fussed him.

'He's being great,' Ellie said. 'Will you get on him today?'

'I'll lean my weight over, but I think I'll give him one more day before I back him properly.'

Ellie felt a flash of impatience but didn't argue. This was Joe's thing. Swapping positions with him, she held the pony while Joe moved round to the left-hand side. Stroking Solo's shoulder, he bent his left leg so Ellie could give him a leg up. He didn't swing all the way into the saddle, but just lay over Solo's back, letting the pony get used to his weight. Solo turned his head to the right and looked at Joe with his ears pricked, as if to say, 'What are you doing there?'

He seemed very relaxed, so after a few minutes Joe asked Ellie to start leading him. They went all the way round the ring with Joe lying across Solo's back and the pony looking extremely calm. When they'd started working with Solo that morning, Ellie had been awkwardly aware of her thoughts from the day before, but with Solo to concentrate on she'd quickly forgotten everything other than working the pony.

'That'll do,' Joe said as they reached the gate again. 'He's been really good.' He slid down from Solo's back.

He and Ellie exchanged pleased looks.

'Do you mind if I go to see Spirit now?' she asked as they walked Solo back to the barn. She wanted to check if his legs were still stiff.

'Sure,' Joe said. 'And don't worry about being late – Dad's asked me and Luke to do the feeds for him this morning.'

Spirit was standing quietly in his stable, one leg resting. He pricked his ears as Ellie came in. She put her arms round him and waited for their minds to connect. As they linked, she felt the same ache in her legs as she'd felt the day before.

You're still hurting, Spirit, she thought in concern. *Should I call the vet?*

No.

Is there anything I can do?

A fuzzy picture of a plant appeared in her mind. Ellie frowned. What did it mean? The image grew sharper. She could see it was a clump of nettles, but she had no idea what that had to do with Spirit's aching legs. Had he stung his legs on some nettles? But she dismissed that thought almost immediately. She was sure nettles didn't sting horses like they did humans. *What do you mean? What are you trying to tell me?*

Spirit gazed at her.

Ellie felt frustrated, but knew that was how communication between them worked – sometimes it was clear; sometimes it wasn't. She ran her hands over his legs. There were no other bumps or rashes, injuries or stings. No reason she could see why his legs might be aching. His fetlocks were slightly warm, but there was no swelling or real heat that would indicate a sprain or injury.

I'm sorry. I don't understand, she thought, feeling useless. *Can't you tell me what the matter is?*

Once again the nettles came into her mind. Why was he showing her them? What did they mean? She stared at him, wishing she could work out what he was trying to tell her.

You'll be OK, won't you? she asked anxiously.

Yes, he told her, just as he had the day before.

Slightly comforted, she buried her head in his silky mane. She wished she could stay in the stable forever.

'Hi there,' Joe greeted her when she finally went into the feedroom. 'How's Spirit?'

'I'm a bit worried about him,' Ellie admitted.

'Why? What's up?'

'He . . .' Ellie stopped herself from saying *told me*. 'He seems a bit stiff.'

'It could have been the jumping yesterday,' Joe said. 'But then we didn't do that much.'

Luke paused in mixing the feeds. 'Is he coughing or are his glands up?'

'No.'

'Any other signs?

'No. Just stiffness.'

Joe shrugged. 'It doesn't sound too bad.'

'You should get him checked out by the vet if you're worried, though,' Luke put in.

Ellie felt surprised; it wasn't like Luke to be serious. 'Do you really think I should get the vet?' she said anxiously.

'I wouldn't worry about it too much. It's probably nothing,' Joe reassured her. 'Just rest him for a few days, and if he's still not right call the vet then.'

'OK,' Ellie said, feeling better. Joe was right; it probably was nothing. Spirit himself had said he would be fine.

Later, when she took Spirit out to the field she watched him carefully. To her relief, he was lively enough to keep pulling her to the side of the track where the grass was long and overgrown. 'Spirit!' she scolded, pulling him back. 'You can eat all the grass you want in the field in a minute!' But she didn't mind really. She was just glad he was so full of energy.

As soon as she took his headcollar off, he trotted down to the fence at the edge of the field and started pawing at the long grass there. He glanced round at her and whinnied.

She smiled, glad he didn't seem too ill. 'See you later!' she called to him and went back to her chores.

Len was in an even more perfectionist mood than usual, with Jeff and Anna Hallett coming to see Lucifer that day. He shouted at Helen and Sasha for not cleaning the tack well enough the day before, scraping his finger down the insides of the bridle to show them the minute traces of grease they had left, and made Joe and Ellie pick up every bit of straw from the courtyard by hand. Everyone kept their heads down and there was very little chatting. Ellie hated it when her uncle was in such a mood. She found it very hard not to fight back. *Remember Spirit, remember Spirit*, she told herself over and over again.

By three o'clock, however, the yard was looking

immaculate with not a strand of straw blowing across it. Rugs were folded neatly over doors and headcollars hung from their hooks outside the stables. Len had told Ellie, Joe and Luke that he wanted all of them there to meet Jeff and Anna – presenting a united front and emphasizing that the yard was a family business.

'It's nice Uncle Len wants them to meet us all,' said Ellie as she and the two boys gathered in the yard.

'It's only because he thinks that if Jeff sees us as a family he might think twice before ever pulling the plug on the sponsorship and taking the money he gives Dad away,' said Joe.

'Oh.' Ellie realized she should have known there was an ulterior motive.

'Well, for the sake of the yard we'd better pretend we're one big, happy family,' said Luke, putting his arm round her shoulders.

She pushed him away. 'Get off!'

'United front, remember?'

Ellie rolled her eyes at him.

'So, are you still planning on going to Westfields with Pericles and Gabriel on Friday, Luke?' Joe broke in quickly.

'Yeah. I was going to take Troy too, but his back needs longer to recover. You still not interested?'

Joe shook his head.

'Westfields?' said Ellie curiously. 'What's that?'

'It's a big equestrian centre about half an hour away,' explained Joe. 'They do indoor winter jumping shows. It's good for the horses to go round a course of jumps outside the main show season. We don't go in to win, just to school them. Hunters don't have to jump off against the clock like show jumpers, so it's more about giving them a practice.'

'Well, I'm not just going there to practise,' said Luke. 'I'm aiming to win.'

'Dad'll kill you if you rush them in the jump-off,' warned Joe.

A smile curved at Luke's lips. 'Then I guess it's good he's not going – there's that evening do at the Halletts', remember, where Jeff gets all the people he sponsors together. I'm going to the show on my own and I'm out to have some fun. Gabriel's got a top jump and he's fast. He'll love it. Thought I'd take him in the speed class too.'

Joe shook his head. 'You're mental.'

'You should bring Barney.'

'No, you know that's not my kind of thing.'

Luke looked at Ellie. 'How about you then? You could ride Barney – or bring Picasso.'

'Me?' Ellie stared.

'Why not? I've seen you jump. That first day you rode here and Len put you on Gabriel, you did four foot. You'd like show jumping.'

Excitement leapt through Ellie. She loved the

thought of going show jumping, but when she glanced at Joe she immediately sensed he didn't want her to go.

She shook her head.

'Why not?'

'It's . . . it's not my thing either.' She saw Joe smile as she echoed his words. Luke, however, gave her a disbelieving look.

'Yeah, right! Since when?'

She was saved from answering by Len's arrival at the courtyard with the Halletts.

Anna was nineteen, very pretty, with long, dark curling hair and brown eyes. She and her dad looked round approvingly at the spotless yard.

'This is my family,' Len introduced them. 'You've met Joe and Luke before, haven't you, Jeff? And this is my niece, Ellie, who's living here now.'

'Hi.' Ellie smiled. But Anna Hallett's eyes swept straight over her as if she was of no more interest than a bug.

Jeff smiled, though. 'Nice to meet you, Ellie.'

'And there's Lucifer,' Len said, pointing to Lucifer who was standing at his stable door, tossing his head.

Anna moved towards him, but Len stopped her. 'I wouldn't, love. He's still unsettled.'

As if to prove Len's point, Lucifer lashed out at the stable wall.

'He seems a bit highly strung,' Jeff Hallett said,

looking warily at the black gelding. 'He wasn't like that when we saw him in the show ring.'

'Don't worry,' Len said confidently. 'He'll soon calm down. He was kept on his own at his old home, so it'll take him a while to get used to being with other horses.' He smiled. 'If he wins in the ring, we'll put up with a few bad stable manners.'

Anna looked at him. 'I want him to qualify for the Horse of the Year Show,' she said, her voice cool. 'Will he?'

Len nodded. 'Absolutely.'

Jeff clapped him on the back. 'Good man! That's what I want to hear. I want to see my Anna in that ring, winning the sash.' He looked affectionately at his daughter.

'So who'll ride him for me when I can't get back from uni for shows?' Anna's eyes glanced between Ellie, Joe and Luke.

'Me,' Luke replied.

Anna looked pleased.

'So, got any other new horses?' Jeff asked Len.

'Aye. A few decent youngsters coming through. A hunter pony called Solo who I'm about to back, and Minstrel, a three-year-old, who I think is going to make a top hack. Come and see them.'

As the two men wandered up the yard, looking at the other horses, Anna moved closer to Luke. 'So *you'll* be riding Lucifer?' Her voice was flirtatious as she looked at him through her dark eyelashes. 'I hope he'll be in good hands.'

'The best. I'll get him to the Horse of the Year show,' Luke told her confidently.

'Unless *I'm* the one who qualifies him,' said Anna. 'After all, I am going to take him in some of the shows myself.' She looked up at him with a challenge. 'Maybe we should see which of us can get a ticket first.'

Luke grinned at her. 'You're on. I like a challenge.' He held her gaze.

Anna blushed and looked down.

Ellie rolled her eyes. Luke couldn't seem to meet a girl without flirting.

'Look, we'll leave you guys to chat,' Joe said to them. 'There's work to do. Come on, Ellie.' She hurried away after him.

As soon as they were out of hearing distance, she imitated Luke. '*I like a challenge!*' She shook her head. 'Honestly! He's not supposed to be flirting with her – your dad said – and what about Sasha? He's supposed to be going out with her.'

Joe shook his head. 'Since when has that ever stopped Luke?'

'I just don't get what everyone sees in him.'

Joe glanced at her. 'I don't know. Maybe it's got something to do with the fact that he's tall, dark, good-looking –'

'Well, I wouldn't go out with him,' Ellie snorted.

Joe looked at her for a moment. 'No.' He smiled suddenly. 'But then you're not like anyone else, Ellie.'

She looked at him with pretend suspicion. 'I hope you mean that in a good way.'

He grinned without answering.

She punched his arm. 'Oi!'

As they reached the pony barn, Joe turned to her suddenly. 'Ellie?'

'What?'

'I was just thinking. We haven't done anything fun for ages. How about going to see a film on Friday night?'

'A film?' Ellie echoed.

'Yeah.'

'Just us?' Ellie felt excitement spark through her.

'Nah, I was thinking of asking Dad, Sasha, Helen, Stu . . . Of course, just us, you idiot.' His face started to close up as if he was already regretting asking. 'Oh, forget it, we're so busy. It was just a mad idea –'

'No!' Ellie interrupted quickly. 'It would be cool. Let's! I haven't seen a film since I came here.'

'OK.' Joe looked pleased. 'It's a date then. I mean, not a date,' he added hastily. 'Just friends going out. You know what I mean.'

'Yeah, yeah . . . of course.' Ellie looked at the ground, hoping he couldn't see her face. When he'd asked, she thought he'd meant a date. She couldn't help feeling a little disappointed, but going out, even just as friends, would be fun.

'We'll have to decide what we want to see,' Joe said.

'No horror,' Ellie said firmly, trying to match his practical tone.

'No slushy movies,' said Joe.

'No movies with talking animals,' declared Ellie.

'Oh, please,' Joe teased. 'Please can't we watch a talking animal?'

'Well . . .' Ellie pretended to consider it. '*No!*'

Laughing together, they went into the barn.

Chapter Six

While Ellie groomed and cleaned tack that afternoon, she kept thinking about Friday night. 'You're in a good mood,' Luke said to her as she practically skipped into the tackroom.

'Yep!' she said, putting her grooming kit away.

'How come?'

'I just am.' She couldn't stop herself; she wanted to share it with someone. 'Joe and I are going to the cinema on Friday.'

'Oh, right.' Luke raised an eyebrow. 'And that's why you're so happy?' He shook his head. 'You seriously need to get out more.'

Ellie just grinned; she wasn't going to let anything dent her excitement.

Just then, Len called Luke's name from the yard. Luke went to the door.

'Give me a hand, will you? I'm going to turn Lucifer out to see if it calms him down.'

'Sure,' Luke said.

Ellie followed them curiously. Whenever a new horse went out for the first time, Len marked out a separate area in the field with electric tape, so the horse could see and sniff the other horses over the tape but have a few days getting to know them before being turned out with them.

Lucifer pranced and jogged on the way to the field, Luke on one side and Len on the other. Hearing him coming, the horses in the field put their heads up and stared enquiringly. Len led Lucifer around the taped off section of field, showing him the tape, the wooden fence and trees along one side, the water trough and the cattle grid that separated his field from the fields behind, left over from when the stables had been a farm in the past. After Len had walked the horse round, he took Lucifer's leadrope off and let him go free.

Merlin came over to Lucifer's paddock first, trotting up to the tape that separated them. Lucifer acted as if he'd been shot. He squealed and thundered at the tape at a gallop. Merlin skidded to a surprised halt.

Ellie gasped – for a moment she thought Lucifer was going to break through the tape or jump it, but he didn't. He simply turned round and kicked out viciously with both hind legs. Merlin backed off with an alarmed snort. The black horse swung round, his ears flat against his head. A few of the other horses, including Spirit, came over and though he didn't seem quite as fierce with them he chased them off too. Every bit of his body language screamed *keep away* as he trotted up and down the fence.

'He thinks he's the boss,' said Len, watching through narrowed eyes. 'We won't ever be putting him and Hereward out together, that's for sure.'

'It'd be like World War Three,' commented Luke.

Ellie nodded. Hereward was the undisputed boss of the geldings.

Len turned to Ellie. 'Can you stay here and watch him for a bit, check he's OK? I've got a client coming for a lesson. Any problems with him, find Stuart or Luke.'

'Sure,' Ellie said. She had no objections to sitting in the sun and watching the horses for a while. It would give her a chance to watch Spirit too and see if he was still stiff.

Len and Luke left. For a long while, the black gelding paced up and down as if daring the other horses to come any closer. It wasn't until they were all a good distance away that he dropped his head and started to graze, taking quick short nervous bites of the grass.

Ellie frowned. She knew her uncle had said Lucifer was a dominant horse, but, watching him now, she wasn't so sure. Underneath the layers of aggression she had the feeling that he was scared, yet a dominant horse surely wouldn't be fearful. Truly dominant horses like Hereward and Starlight were always brave and confident characters. That wasn't how Lucifer seemed to her at all. She could almost feel the anxiety radiating off him. His aggression seemed designed to keep people – and other horses – away.

What's going on in his head?

Maybe she could find out. She'd planned on talking to a different horse – well, why not Lucifer?

Perhaps I can help him. Looking at the black horse, she made up her mind. As soon as she had the chance she would speak to him.

Ellie's opportunity came after supper. Joe went off to revise for his exams, Luke was watching TV and Len went out to meet a client. Ellie slipped out of the kitchen.

All the horses were in their stables and the night sky lit up with stars. A cat trotted through the shadows and there was a snort from one of the stables. Lucifer was staring out over his door, moving restlessly from side to side.

'Hey, boy,' Ellie murmured, going closer. Lucifer shook his head at her warningly. Ellie tried to reach out to him just as she had with Troy. *It's OK*, she told him, sending him waves of love. *I'm not going to hurt you. You can talk to me.* She waited confidently, expecting to feel the shift in the atmosphere, but nothing happened.

Speak to me, she urged him. *I'm here. I'll listen.*

He pinned his ears back and Ellie frowned. Ignoring his hostility, she went closer. *Come on. You can talk to me, fella.*

Lucifer retreated into his stable. She could feel he wanted to be left alone but she was determined to talk to him.

Lucifer, it's OK. But Lucifer just stayed at the back of his stall, his hindquarters facing her. It was clear he didn't want to talk. Eventually, frustrated, she gave up and went to find Spirit.

He whickered softly to her. Letting herself into his stable, she told him what she'd been doing.

Ellie felt encouragement flowing from him. *Just listen. Be patient. Wait*, he said.

I did wait and I did listen, but he didn't speak.

Spirit sent a picture of her and Lucifer together. In the image, she was standing a little way off and the black gelding looked calm and peaceful. She was talking to him. *You can do it*, Spirit told her.

But how?

The picture grew brighter but nothing happened in it. Ellie felt sure she wasn't understanding the message. She sighed, wanting a solution that was easy to understand. Putting her arms round his neck, she hugged him and he nuzzled her back.

It's OK, don't worry, she told him. *I'll figure it out. So how are you feeling now, Spirit? How are your legs?*

She felt the ache again in her own calves and ankles.

They still hurt?

Yes.

A clump of nettles sprang into her mind again. Ellie pushed the image of the plant away. She really had no idea why he kept showing her nettles, but she wanted to concentrate on the ache. *Is it here?* she said, touching his fetlocks.

Yes.

She stroked his legs, wishing she could help. He nuzzled her. *You were happy earlier today*, he said.

She straightened up and smiled. *Yes. It's Joe. We're going out together on Friday night. It'll be fun.* She found herself wondering how Joe was feeling about it.

She put her arms round Spirit's neck and kissed him. It was all so much easier with him.

Luke was in the kitchen making coffee when she finally went in. Pip was snuffling round the floor. 'Where have you been?' he asked curiously.

She sat down to take her boots off. 'I just went to see Spirit.'

'How is he? Still stiff?'

Ellie blinked, surprised Luke had remembered about Spirit's stiffness. 'Yes.'

'I know what Joe said, but you should get the vet out if you're worried,' Luke told her. 'You've got to trust your instincts with horses. Do you feel you should call the vet?'

'I don't know,' she admitted.

'Well, if you start thinking you should, then do it,' said Luke. 'I had a pony called Maggie when I was ten. I knew she wasn't OK one night, I just knew it, but Dad and our groom said she was fine. We all left the stables. Turned out I was the one who was right. Maggie had colic and she got bad quickly after we'd all left. The groom found her when he did the late-night check. She'd been rolling and had twisted her gut.'

Ellie caught her breath.

Luke nodded as he saw her reaction. 'Yeah. They tried to operate but she had to be put down.' His jaw tightened. 'Anyway, it's not important. But my advice is if you're worried about Spirit, get him checked out. Don't just ignore it.'

Ellie nodded. 'I will. Thanks.' She didn't quite know what to say. 'That's an awful thing to have happened, Luke.'

He shrugged. 'It was a long time ago.'

Ellie had never heard him talk about his past before. She wanted to ask him more, but he'd picked up his coffee and was already heading through to the lounge.

Ellie didn't forget what he'd said, though, and when her uncle arrived home she asked if she could call the vet the next day. Len listened and then nodded. 'The vet's coming tomorrow afternoon to give Lucifer a check over. He can have a look at that grey of yours at the same time. You're right to want to call him.' Ellie was surprised that Len was so keen to get the vet until he added, 'After all, it could be a virus and in that case we don't want him near the other horses. We need to find out for sure.'

Ellie sighed. She should have known better than to think her uncle cared about Spirit. It was all to do with his precious show horses! Still, she felt happier knowing that at least the vet would be checking Spirit over.

He'll be OK, she told herself as she went to bed later. *He said he would be*. But with Luke's story in her mind, she found it hard to sleep that night.

The next morning, Ellie got up even earlier than Joe and went to check Spirit before they started working with Solo.

He sent her a picture of a clump of nettles again.

She sighed. 'I'm sorry, Spirit. I just don't know what you mean, but hopefully if there's anything wrong the vet will find out.'

She gave him a hug, then went to join Joe and Solo. She felt light and happy as she hurried across the courtyard, really looking forward to seeing how Solo was that day. Joe was just leading the pony out of the barn. Ellie joined them. 'Hi! So, will you ride him today?' she asked. 'Properly sit up and everything?'

Joe nodded. 'Provided he's as good as yesterday.'

Solo was. It only took him a few minutes to join-up with Joe, then he stood calmly as Joe put on his saddle and bridle and experimented with leaning his weight over the pony's back. Finally, Joe got on and slowly sat up. Solo's eyes looked slightly nervous as he caught sight of Joe sitting on his back, but Joe stroked him and patted him and soon the pony was fine. Ellie led him round, then Joe rode him on his own. Solo didn't buck once.

'He's being great!' Ellie said as Joe finally halted beside her.

Joe's eyes glowed. 'I know. I can't remember the number of times I've been bucked off horses and ponies when Dad's been backing them. This is the way it should be done!' He dismounted and patted Solo. 'Look at him, there's no fear in his eyes. No stress. We'll have to do it like this all the time from now on. Help as many horses as we can!'

'Definitely!' she said, caught in his enthusiasm. 'You can join-up with them and I'll help you. We'll do it together!'

He grinned and pulled her into a hug. As she felt the rough material of his sweatshirt against her face and his arms round her, everything she had been thinking about in the last few days suddenly bubbled up and she couldn't stop the words from coming out.

'Joe? Do you ever think about what happened in the horsebox?' She pulled back slightly to see his face. 'When we almost . . . almost . . .'

The atmosphere suddenly changed, the closeness between them replaced by tension. 'I know.' Joe stepped away from her.

She watched him, half nervous, half excited. What was he going to say?

He swallowed. 'I've actually been thinking about it a lot, Els.'

'And?' She held her breath, her heart starting to race.

Joe pushed a hand through his hair. 'And . . .' He hesitated, his eyes on hers. 'We just can't do things like that.'

She felt a crashing sense of anti-climax. It was so not what she'd expected him to say. 'You . . . you mean you don't *want* to?' she stammered.

'It's not that I don't want to,' he answered swiftly. 'But we're cousins. Dad would flip –'

'We could keep it secret!' Ellie burst out.

'It would never stay secret. You know it wouldn't. Someone would find out. And . . . we just shouldn't.'

Ellie stared at him. She knew what he was like, how he liked to please people, how he hated rows. But the more he said no, the more certain she felt that it was what she wanted. 'If we want it, we shouldn't just give up. You *do* like me?'

He looked torn. 'Yes. Of course I do – so much.'

'Well, I like you so couldn't . . . couldn't we just try?'

But even as she spoke, she saw the resignation in his eyes. He was shaking his head.

Ellie felt tears well up. Not wanting him to see how upset she was, she swung round and started to hurry away.

'Ellie! Wait!'

Taking a breath to calm herself, she stopped and turned.

Joe was looking at her pleadingly. 'This doesn't have to change anything. We can still be friends, can't we?'

She hesitated, but couldn't imagine them not being friends and so she nodded. 'Yes.' Her throat hurt with the tears she was holding back. 'Though you're wrong about this,' she said stubbornly. 'I know you are.'

Turning on her heel, she walked on. This time he didn't call her back.

Chapter Seven

Ellie went straight to Spirit. Reaching the sanctuary of his stable, she put her arms round his neck. The words tumbled out of her as she told him what had just happened. She wasn't sure how much he understood about boy and girl stuff but it was enough he knew she was upset. She felt the waves of comfort coming from him and gradually her feelings calmed. She sighed and, resting her head against his neck, replayed the conversation with Joe in her head. It was almost impossible to believe that Joe had completely given up the idea of them being together. They really were so perfect for each other.

I'm not going to give up, she thought, feeling a rush of determination. *I'm right about this and Joe will see it in the end. I know he will.*

By the time Ellie went to help with the feeds, she felt back in control. She would give Joe some time. If he liked her and she liked him, surely he was going to change his mind and they could become boyfriend and girlfriend in the end. All she had to do was wait. Admittedly she never found waiting easy but she was going to try,

She felt a bit awkward as she went into the feed-room and saw Joe, but with Len and Luke both there too, she quickly slipped back into acting normally. She and Joe didn't have much chance to talk; they were both too busy with the usual morning chores. But they did meet up by the muck heap when Luke rode Lucifer for the first time. Wanting to watch, Ellie grabbed a broom, only to arrive at the muck heap and find Joe had done the same. Realizing they'd had the same thought, they smiled awkwardly.

'Great minds think alike.' Joe spoke lightly, but Ellie knew him well enough to read the uncertainty in his eyes.

'I couldn't miss this.' She smiled at him and instantly he looked relieved, glad she wasn't in a mood with him.

Luke led Lucifer up to the ring. The gelding sidled and jogged like a racehorse in the paddock. Sasha walked alongside, talking constantly to Luke, but his attention was completely on the tense horse, his hands firm on the reins. Len was waiting by the gate.

'Good luck,' Sasha called as Luke reached the gate.

'Luck's got nothing to do with it,' Len said brusquely from the ring. 'Riding well is what counts.'

Ellie could see the excitement in Luke's eyes. She knew she would have felt exactly the same if she'd been about to prove herself capable of riding Lucifer in the ring.

Luke swung himself easily into the saddle. The gelding immediately plunged forward, but Luke kept his seat and moved with him. Clicking his tongue, he gathered the reins and started to trot him round in circles.

Ellie watched, wondering if there would be a fight, but to her relief Lucifer settled down quickly. He was soon on the bit, his neck arched, his smooth stride effortlessly covering the ground. He was beautiful to watch and Ellie could see why he had won so much during his first year in the show ring. He was very responsive, and Luke barely had to move in the saddle as he rode him in figures of eight and serpentines.

'Look at him,' said Joe admiringly as he and Ellie swept, keeping their eyes on the ring. 'He's got real star quality.'

Both Luke and Len were soon smiling. Eventually, Luke brought the horse to a halt and patted him, then Len mounted. He rode as a judge in the ring would, his reins slightly long and hands light, seeing how responsive the horse was. Lucifer went just as easily for him.

'There,' he said, when he finally stopped him. 'I said he'd calm down and be just fine.' He clapped the horse's neck. 'Good lad.'

'Should I take him down the lane to cool him off?' Luke asked.

Len nodded and dismounted. 'Then he can go out in the field again.'

'Well, that went better than expected,' Joe said to Ellie as Luke patted the horse too and led him out of the ring.

Ellie watched Lucifer. In the menage he had seemed fairly calm and relaxed, but as Luke led him back towards the yard he tensed up. His ears flickered back and forward and he started to jog and sidle. *Why?* Ellie thought to herself. Most horses walked eagerly out of the school, pleased to have finished work. She leant on her broom. She just couldn't figure Lucifer out. She wished he had talked to her.

Just listen. Spirit's words came to her as she watched Lucifer being led into his stable.

I tried that, she thought in frustration. *But as he didn't talk to me, I had nothing to listen to!* If only Spirit had given her some other clue about what to do.

John Taylor, the vet, arrived just before lunch in his battered four-wheel drive. He was an experienced vet in his fifties. After checking Lucifer over and finding him in good health, John turned his attention to Spirit.

'So, what's up with him?' he asked Ellie as they walked to the stable.

'He's been stiff for the last few days. I think his fetlocks are hurting him,' said Ellie.

At first, Spirit was nervous. He was still wary of strangers, particularly men. But his trust in Ellie was obvious, and while she held and soothed him he let John listen to his heart, examine him and check his legs. After Ellie had trotted him up and down so John could see his movement, the vet looked thoughtful. 'Well, there's nothing definite,' he said as Stuart came over to join them and see what he thought. 'Spirit's a little stiff, as you say. At his age and with his past . . .' He looked at Spirit assessingly. 'I'd say it's likely he's got a degenerative joint problem – a touch of arthritis.'

Ellie frowned. 'Arthritis?'

'Yes, I'm afraid there's nothing you can do about it, love. It's just old age and wear and tear, but there's also no need to panic.' John's eyes were kindly as he saw her face. 'If you manage it carefully, he'll probably be fine for quite a few years to come. Keep exercising him and turning him out – rest him if the ground is particularly hard or if he looks especially stiff. If it gets worse let me know and I'll investigate further. We'll probably have to consider pain relief in the future, but he should be OK for now.'

Ellie nodded, feeling torn between relief that there wasn't anything badly wrong and worry about what it would mean. 'Is there anything else I can do?'

'You could add cod liver oil to his feed. That's a traditional remedy.'

'Equi-Glow do several supplements for joint problems,' Stuart told Ellie. 'We can use one of those. There's a nettle and dandelion one –'

'Nettles?' Ellie interrupted.

Stuart nodded. 'I know it sounds odd, but they're good for arthritis. And horses seem to know that. You'll often see older horses graze on them if there are any in their field – although a lot of horses will only eat them if they've been picked and left on the ground.'

So that was why Spirit had been showing her nettles! Ellie was dumbfounded. She stared at Spirit. He looked back patiently.

All along, you were trying to show me what you needed, she thought.

She became aware that Stuart was talking to her about the different supplements that were available. She smiled and nodded, but was too busy watching Spirit to pay much attention. How could she have ignored his messages so completely?

As soon as she could she took him to his stall and, although it was the afternoon and there were things to do, she locked herself in his stable and opened her mind to his.

Spirit, I'm so sorry, she told him quickly. *All the time you kept showing me the nettles – you tried to take me to them*, she said, remembering how he had pulled her to the side of the path. *But I just didn't get it. Deep down I knew there had to be a reason why you kept showing me nettles, but I couldn't work it out so I just decided to ignore you.*

Spirit sent her a wave of love.

She stared at him. There wasn't even a hint of reproach. She had ignored him but he wasn't blaming her.

You should be mad with me.

She sensed his confusion. It was as if he couldn't understand the thought. She suddenly realized that to him it didn't matter that she hadn't listened. He didn't blame her the way a human might have done. All she felt from him was relief now she knew what he meant – and the same love as always. She swallowed. Horses were amazing. They didn't lie, they didn't blame – all they asked for was to be treated kindly, and that made them content. She hugged him. A picture of some nettles came into her mind and Spirit nudged her gently with his nose.

Ellie took the hint and smiled. There was no way she would ignore him again. *OK. I'll fetch some now.*

Still thinking about it all, Ellie went out and found some gloves and secateurs, then returned ten minutes later with a bucketful of nettles. She put them on the straw and Spirit started to eat them. It was amazing when she thought how hard he had been trying to communicate what he wanted.

'I'll listen next time you tell me something,' she whispered. 'Oh, Spirit, I promise I will.'

Chapter Eight

On Friday, Joe was competing in an Easter show on Wisp, a young show hunter pony. Three of the liveries were entered too, so Joe and Len were out for the whole day. Ellie enjoyed riding without her every move being watched, and at lunchtime she took Spirit out for a hack. Since the vet's visit, she had picked nettles for him twice a day and Stuart had found an Equi-Glow supplement that was particularly good for horses with arthritis. There might be no cure but she wanted to make sure Spirit's aches and pains were eased as much as possible.

It was lovely being out with him; they ambled along the lane and stopped to look down the mountainside. The sun was shining and lambs were bouncing around the fields. Ellie leant forward, putting her arms round Spirit's neck. There was no place she would rather be. Her thoughts skipped forward to that night when she and Joe would go to the cinema.

Would the evening end with her feeling as happy as she was now?

Maybe. After all, despite everything Joe had said, he did like her. She wondered if he was also thinking about the night ahead while he was at the show. Smiling to herself, she sat up, touched her heels to Spirit's sides and rode on.

When she got back, she decided to groom Merlin. She knew Joe would be pleased and so she brushed the little bay pony with the body brush until his coat shone. She even oiled his hooves and put a tail bandage on his tail. He seemed to love the fuss, nuzzling her shoulder as she put a final polish on his coat by smoothing over him with a cactus cloth.

As she stood back to admire him, Luke brought Gabriel and Pericles on to the yard and started preparing them for the evening's indoor jumping show. Sasha was helping him.

'I could come with you tonight,' the elder girl offered, a little too hopefully.

'Don't worry. I'll be fine,' Luke told her. 'It's just a jumping show.'

'But –'

'Nah, don't worry, babe. I'll manage.'

Sasha obviously wanted to go, and pouted, but Luke took no notice.

Ellie wondered if things were cooling between

them. It wouldn't surprise her. After all, they'd lasted almost a month – a record by Luke's standards.

At five o'clock all the grooms left. Sasha flounced off, barely saying goodbye to Luke. He didn't seem bothered, though, as he packed up the small horsebox.

Ellie was just doing a final check of the water buckets for the evening when she heard Joe returning. She went to help unload the horses.

'How did it go?' she called, reaching the car park as Joe got out of the cab.

'Great. Wisp won. Fizz got a second, Bill got a fourth and Darcey won her class and the championship.'

They both helped to put the horses and ponies away, rugging them up and feeding them.

'So, what time are we leaving?' Ellie finally asked Joe, trying to sound casual, as they carried the last two saddles to the tackroom.

Joe looked awkward. 'Um . . . I need to talk to you about that.'

'Why?'

Just then, the house door opened. Len stood in the doorway, wearing smart trousers. 'Get yourself moving, Joe. We need to be gone in ten minutes.' He went back inside.

Ellie looked at Joe. 'Gone? Where are you going?'

'Look, I'm sorry, Ellie.' Joe looked a bit embarrassed. 'But Dad wants me to go with him to Jeff Hallett's party tonight. All the people that Equi-Glow sponsors are supposed to be there. I don't want to, but Dad thinks we should keep up the united family front.' He saw her face. 'I really should go, Els. I'm sorry. I hadn't realized Dad would expect me to.'

Ellie stared at him. 'Why don't you just tell him you can't? Tell him you're busy – that you're already doing something with me?'

Joe shook his head. 'I can't. The sponsorship is so important to the yard. It would be wrong of me not to go.' He looked appeasingly at her. 'You understand, don't you? It's only a film we're missing. We can go another time.' He turned to the house. 'Are you coming in?'

Ellie shook her head. 'No . . . not just yet.' She felt as if he had just dumped a bucket of cold water all over her.

'OK. Well, I'll catch you later.' Joe hurried inside.

Ellie walked slowly to Spirit's stall. Suddenly her secret hopes seemed mad.

Reaching Spirit's stall, she hugged him until she heard the house door bang. 'Ellie!' Joe was calling faintly for her. 'Ellie!' She didn't answer.

After a few minutes, she heard his footsteps as he came to find her. 'I'm off.' His hair was brushed and he'd changed into smart clothes. 'I'll see you later. I have to go. I'm sorry I can't go to the movies.'

Not sorry enough to stay, Ellie thought, still hurting, but trying to hide it. 'Sure. See you later,' she shrugged.

'Yeah. Later.'

Joe hurried away, leaving her feeling worse than ever. He hadn't even realized she was upset. A few minutes afterwards she heard the sound of the car engine revving.

Ellie felt like kicking the stable wall, but instead she stroked Spirit. 'I'd better get something to eat,' she sighed. 'I'll come and see you afterwards.'

She set off towards the house.

'Thought you were going out tonight?' Luke said, as he led Gabriel out on to the yard in his travelling boots and lightweight rug.

'Yeah. Me too,' muttered Ellie.

'Where's Joe then?'

'Gone to Jeff Hallett's with Len.'

Luke looked at her incredulously. 'You've been stood up for Jeff Hallett! Oh, that's good!' He started to grin.

'Not stood up,' Ellie rushed in defensively. 'Joe had to go.'

Luke spluttered. 'He didn't *have* to go. He could have said no. I mean, it's going to be full of oldies. No one expects him to be there. He could have talked Len out of it if he'd wanted to. But I guess it was his famous sense of duty kicking in.'

Ellie turned away swiftly. She didn't need Luke echoing the thoughts that were in her head. She was cross enough with Joe as it was, but she didn't want to criticize him with Luke. She continued towards the house.

'Hey, Ellie! Wait up!'

'What?' she said miserably.

'Why don't you come to the horse show with me this evening? You could take Gabriel in a class.'

Ellie stared. 'I couldn't do that!'

Luke shrugged. 'Why not?'

Ellie opened her mouth. There were all sorts of reasons why not. For a start, what would her uncle say? And she'd only ridden Gabriel once before – how could she possibly take him in a show-jumping competition? But looking into Luke's blue eyes, she realized that to him there really was no reason why she couldn't go to the show if she wanted. He just didn't see obstacles the way most people did. She felt a surge of wonderful excitement.

'Well?' he went on. 'If you want to, you can. You'll need your show clothes, though.'

A smile caught at her lips. She would do what she wanted this time. 'OK, I'll come!'

The car park at the show was lit up by big floodlights. Luke parked the lorry and they jumped out. People were unloading horses, fixing tendon boots.

The pony classes had already been on and ponies were being loaded back into horseboxes, riders wearing Puffa jackets over their show clothes to keep warm and clean.

'Let's see what class is on now,' Luke said.

Weaving through the crowds, they headed for the indoor school where the competition was taking place. They walked into a cafe where the smell of hot dogs, sawdust and frying onions filled the air, with people sitting on the red plastic seats holding polystyrene cups of coffee as they watched the jumping. One wall was glass and Ellie could see a steel-grey horse jumping round a course in the school. Luke checked with a pretty red-haired girl with a ponytail behind the counter. 'What class is it, Jodie?'

'The Novice Jumping.' Jodie smiled at him. 'I was wondering if you would be here today, Luke. I haven't seen you for a month or two.'

'Been missing me?'

'Maybe, maybe not.' But Jodie's blush gave it away.

'I've missed *you*.'

Ellie rolled her eyes. Honestly! Couldn't Luke go anywhere without flirting? She wondered if Jodie was the reason Luke hadn't wanted Sasha at the show. Luke caught her expression. 'This is Ellie, by the way, Jodie. She's Joe's cousin and she's living with us now.'

'Oh, right.' Jodie looked Ellie up and down.

Luke headed for the door. 'Come on,' he said over his shoulder to Ellie.

Ellie folded her arms. 'Excuse me?'

When he didn't look round, she followed him. 'I'm not Pip, you know!' she hissed.

'What do you mean?'

Ellie spoke indignantly. 'Ordering me around like that.'

Luke grinned. 'Why do you always have to argue? Come on, quit with the mood. We're at a show. Let's enter you in a class.' He strode off.

'Luke!' Ellie ran after him. Now they were there, the reality of the situation was starting to sink in. 'I really can't go in a class.'

'Why not?' Luke's eyes searched hers. 'You want to, don't you?'

'Well, yeah,' Ellie admitted. She desperately wanted a chance to jump. 'Of course I do but –'

'Then do it.'

'But –'

'Listen to yourself! You've been spending too much time with Joe. But this . . . but that . . .' Luke imitated. He spread his arms. 'Who cares about buts? Look, there's the secretary's office.' He bounded up the steps into the small wooden shed where people entered the classes and collected their numbers. Before Ellie could stop him, he was fishing some money out of his pocket and entering her and Gabriel in the Gamblers' Stakes.

She stood there open-mouthed. 'You're crazy, Luke!' she said, unable to stop herself from smiling as he jumped back down the steps and handed her a number.

He grinned. 'Nope. You're the crazy one. You're going to be taking Gabriel in the Gamblers' Stakes!' Chuckling, he strode back to the horsebox.

There were four jumping classes for the horses. The main jumping classes were the Novice, Intermediate and Open Jumping. Luke was taking both horses in the Open Jumping. The final class of the night was the Gamblers' Stakes, a class where each rider had to jump round the ring for two minutes, collecting points for every fence they jumped, with the hardest and biggest fences having the most points attached. The rider with the most points won.

'How do you think the horses will do?' Ellie asked as they tacked up.

'Oh, I'm not going to jump Pericles fast. He really is just here for the experience,' Luke replied. 'He's not a speed horse and it wouldn't be fair.'

'What about Gabriel?' said Ellie.

'He's totally different. He could have been a show jumper. The problem is stopping him once he's in the ring.'

'Oh, great!' Ellie groaned, her stomach turning somersaults.

'You'll be fine!' Luke told her airily. 'Just point him at the jumps and hang on. He'll do the rest!'

Both horses were on their toes, sidling around as Ellie and Luke mounted. Standing at 15.2 hands high, Gabriel was taller than Ellie was used to, and with his head up and his hocks – his back legs – underneath him he felt as if he'd grown a couple more inches. 'Steady, boy,' she soothed, stroking his neck as he jogged towards the working-in area. Used to Luke's heavier weight and stronger hands, Gabriel pulled at the bit. Ellie murmured to him. She wished she could take him somewhere quiet and try connecting with him, talk to him, but with Luke there it was impossible to slip away.

The working-in ring was full of horses cantering round or going over the practice jumps in the centre of the ring. Occasionally, grooms would risk their lives to dart across the ring and tighten a noseband or fix a boot. As Ellie began to trot Gabriel round he snatched at his bit, but soon he began to settle down. When she felt he had calmed down enough, she turned him towards the practice fence. Instantly, his ears pricked and he plunged forward. Grabbing hold of his plaits, it was all she could do to cling on and use her legs as he raced at the fence. He cleared it by miles, making her fly up from the saddle.

'Whoa!' she gasped. She pulled him into a circle

and slowed him down. Her heart was pounding but her eyes were shining. What a jump!

'Having fun yet?' Luke grinned as he cantered steadily over the jump on Pericles and rode up beside her.

She grinned. 'You bet!'

Pericles jumped a steady clear round in the Open Jumping but there was nothing steady about Gabriel's round. Luke raced him over the course, but to Ellie's delight he went clear. She threw her arms round the horse as Luke halted, patting his neck. 'He's in the jump-off,' she said, feeding him polos.

The jump-off was for the ten horses who had all gone clear, and was a timed event – the fastest round with the fewest faults would win. Pericles jumped clear again, but Luke stuck to his word and didn't rush him. With Gabriel it was a different matter. Riding superbly, Luke galloped him round the course and cut inside fences in a way that no one else dared to do, almost seeming to lift the horse over fences. As they approached the last jump, a wide parallel, Luke pushed Gabriel into a gallop. Ellie held her breath. They were almost home! Gabriel reached the fence but was just too far off. He caught the back pole with his hooves as he landed. It bounced to the ground. Four faults.

'Damn!' said Luke as he rode out, but his eyes

were exhilarated. 'If we'd have nailed that last fence we'd have won by miles. God, what a round!'

No one else came close to Luke's time, but there were five clear rounds in the jump-off so in the end Pericles was fifth and Gabriel sixth. Luke went into the ring on Pericles, leading Gabriel, to collect his two rosettes. When he came out he stuffed them carelessly into his jacket pocket.

'Don't do that, you'll crease them,' Ellie told him.

'So?' Luke laughed. 'I'm not going to keep them. Who cares about a fifth and sixth rosette – winning's what counts.' He patted Gabriel's neck. 'Next time . . .'

At the indoor school the course was being re-arranged for the Gamblers' Stakes. When it was ready, Ellie walked round it on foot to work out the route she would take. The jumps looked very big compared to the ones she had jumped on Picasso in the working hunter pony class. She noticed a couple of easy fences, but jumping those wouldn't win the competition. Her eyes were drawn to the fences that carried the most points. First, there was a big double with two wide spreads, then an imposing upright fence made of bright green and white planks, and finally a massive red wall that was worth twice as many points as anything else. Ellie walked up to it. She could barely see over the top. Could she really jump it?

For a moment she wondered what Joe would say

if he'd been there. She could almost hear him telling her not to even try it, that it would be stupid.

She hesitated, then walked back to the collecting ring where Luke was holding Gabriel. 'You ready for this?' he asked.

She took a deep breath. 'Oh, yes.' She couldn't wait to get into the ring. The atmosphere of the show had taken her over. Stroking Gabriel's warm neck, she watched as the first competitor was called in.

When it was her turn Ellie rode into the ring, her heart in her mouth. Gabriel was excited to be in there again. The seated area was now full with people and she could hear Gabriel's snorts echoing through the quiet air as she rode round, waiting for the bell to tell her to start.

Just keep jumping, she thought, excitement gripping her.

Be sensible, she heard Joe's voice again in her head. She pushed it away.

Luke was standing in the cafe. He grinned and gave her a thumbs-up and she grinned back. The next minute the bell was ringing out and she was off. Gabriel raced towards the first jump – a small spread, then over the gate, the parallel bars and then the big double. All thought of being sensible had vanished from her mind now. She turned Gabriel again and again, facing him at the fences, aware of the points racking up. The urge to win was beating through her, the desire to jump faster, bigger . . .

Suddenly she found herself at the top of the ring with the choice between the wall and the small spread again. She didn't hesitate. Gabriel thundered towards the wall. Ellie had never jumped anything so big in her life. It loomed in front of her, red, white and massive. She held her breath as Gabriel sank back on to his hocks and then he was soaring through the air, clearing it easily. It felt like a lifetime before they landed and she tensed, waiting for the fall of bricks, but there was nothing apart from the sweet sound of his hooves as he cantered on. She'd done it! Elation surged through her, and in the final seconds she turned towards the double and flew over both fences one more time, landing just as the bell rang to end her round.

Gasping for breath, eyes shining, patting Gabriel over and over again, she rode out of the ring. Luke leapt over the fence to meet her. 'God, no one else has even attempted the wall.' He looked amused and impressed. 'That was awesome, Ellie!'

Slithering off, she threw her arms round Gabriel. 'He was brilliant!' She felt like she had fireworks going off inside her.

'Told you – I knew you'd enjoy it.'

Ellie enjoyed the moment when she went into the ring to collect the red first-place rosette even more. She led the lap of honour and cantered out, feeling as if every cell in her body was buzzing. She was so glad she'd listened to Luke and gone to the show, so glad she'd just gone ahead and done it. Whatever happened, whatever trouble she got in, she'd always have that night. It was the same as when she'd bought Spirit. She knew she shouldn't have done it, but she hadn't listened to that sensible bit of her brain and was so glad she hadn't.

'So, it makes up for not going out tonight?' Luke said as they led Gabriel back to the lorry.

'Definitely! I loved it!'

'Knew you would.' He tapped his nose. 'See, I know everything.'

'Yeah, yeah,' she teased, rolling her eyes. 'You know *everything*.'

'I do, babe.'

'Babe?' She looked at him and then burst out laughing, on such a high she simply couldn't be bothered to be angry with him. 'You called me babe!'

He had the good grace to look a bit ashamed. 'OK, sorry, you are so not a babe.'

'What am I then?' she said curiously.

'A nut-job! You must be, you took Gabriel in the Gamblers' Stakes and won.'

Their eyes met and they grinned. Ellie walked Gabriel back to the horsebox, glowing inside.

Chapter Nine

They drove back to High Peak Stables, the radio playing old rock songs. It wasn't Ellie's usual choice of music but it felt right somehow, driving back in the dark with the flickering lights around them, the lorry heater blasting warmth out. She glanced across at Luke whose eyes were fixed on the road. Some days he utterly infuriated her, and then at other times, like now, she really, really liked him. She thought how little she knew about him and his life before he came to live at the stables. The story he'd told her the other night about his pony dying had taken her completely by surprise.

'Did you always have ponies when you were growing up?' she asked, curious to know more.

He nodded. 'Since I was five. My dad used to go hunting a bit and we had stables at our house. I show-jumped quite a lot whenever I was at home.'

Ellie remembered what Joe had once told her –

that Luke's parents were wealthy and he had gone to boarding school from the age of eight.

'Didn't you miss your ponies when you went to boarding school?' She couldn't imagine it.

'Loads. I didn't see them much at all really. I was at school in term time and then quite often I came here in the holidays because my parents were off travelling.'

'So you didn't see much of your parents either?'

Luke shook his head.

'What did they think about you leaving to come here?' Ellie asked, intrigued.

Luke frowned. 'What is this? Twenty questions?' But he answered anyway. 'They didn't have a choice, I guess.' He shrugged. 'Once I'd spoken to Len and knew he'd have me, then there was no way I'd have stayed on at school. I told Dad I'd just run away. He knew I meant it so he let me come here. I think he was secretly glad – a problem ticked off his list.' Luke ticked the air with his hand. 'Luke – dealt with. I'd always been in trouble at school – got myself expelled twice.' He gave a self-mocking smile. '"A cry for attention", that's what the experts said. I reckon it was just me being a bit of a sod.'

Ellie studied his face. Despite his flippant words, she could sense a lot of hurt, deep down. 'Do you get on with your dad?' she asked curiously.

'I don't see him to get on with. Never really have. Even when I was at home in the holidays with him he was always working. He'd watch me riding if he was around and I'd go hunting with him if he wanted to do that, but doing anything else with me – well, that just didn't happen.'

'What about your mum?'

'She runs around after him. Dad's her life. She's never been the sitting-with-you-when-you're-sick, reading-stories-to-you type of mum anyway. More the going-to-the-tanning-salon, having-your-nails-done and going-to-dinner-parties mum. She's not into horses at all.' Luke snorted. 'Really great parents I have. Still, least they're not short of cash and they've never been stingy about spending money on me.' He smiled at her. 'It could have been worse.'

Ellie found it hard to smile back but she felt a wave of sympathy for Luke. It must be awful to grow up like that, feeling unloved by your parents.

Luke tapped his fingers on the steering wheel and gave her a quick glance. 'I know you don't like Len but he's been more of a father to me than my own dad ever has. Least you know where you are with him and though he might shout and roar, it's only because he cares about what you're doing.'

Ellie snorted. 'You mean, he cares that we're riding the horses right! He doesn't care about us!'

Luke shrugged. 'He's been good to me.'

Ellie frowned. 'He's a useless dad to Joe and he *doesn't* care about us. You know he doesn't.' She thought of the nights when she had first arrived at High Peak Stables, the times she had cried herself to sleep. He had never once – not once – asked her how she was. Not only that, but he was so unpredictable there was no knowing what he might do.

'He took us in,' Luke reminded her.

'Only because we could ride the ponies for him,' Ellie shot back. 'There's nothing good about him.'

Luke looked at her for a moment and then to her surprise he laughed. 'You argue too much, Ellie Carrington. OK, OK, you're right. He's a crap dad and a crap person. Happy now?'

Ellie shot him a sideways look. 'Yep. As long as you admit I'm right, I won't argue.'

Luke grinned at her. 'You know, when you first arrived, I thought you were going to be just some silly girl.' He shook his head. 'Wrong!'

Ellie glanced at him curiously. 'So what do you think of me now?'

Luke's forehead furrowed. He gave her an assessing look for a moment before turning back to the road. 'You're interesting.'

Interesting. Ellie sat back against her seat. Well, she didn't object to that. She smiled to herself and they drove the rest of the way home in an easy silence.

When they got back, Ellie saw Len's car in the car park. She and Luke unloaded the horses and led them on to the yard. As she came out of Gabriel's box, she saw Joe coming out of the house. Happiness swept through her – she couldn't wait to tell him all about it, to ease his guilt for going out with his dad that night and cancelling their outing. 'Hi!' she called, hurrying over to him.

'Ellie! I've been worried about you. I didn't realize you were at the show with Luke. When I got back and found you weren't here I didn't know where you'd gone. I've been calling and texting your mobile. Why didn't you answer?'

'My phone's out of charge so I had it switched off.' Her excitement burst out of her. 'Joe, listen! It was brilliant! I took Gabriel in the Gamblers' Stakes. We won!'

He stared. 'You what?'

'We won!'

'You took Gabriel in the Gamblers' Stakes?' he echoed. 'But that was mad. You've only ridden him once.'

'Yeah, I know. But, Joe, we won.' She hugged the travelling wraps to her and relived the experience. 'It was amazing. He went so fast and we jumped the wall – no one else did. It was . . .' Her words faded as she realized he was stony-faced.

'I thought you said you didn't want to go to the show. It didn't take Luke long to persuade you otherwise, did it?'

It was Ellie's turn to stare. 'Sorry?'

Joe frowned. 'You said it wasn't your thing.'

'Joe, you were the one who cancelled tonight. I went to the show with Luke cos you weren't here. I thought you'd be pleased I'd had a good time. I wouldn't have gone at all if you'd stayed.'

'I had to go out.'

'Luke said you didn't.'

Joe's face tightened. 'Oh, I see, *Luke* said . . .'

Looking hurt, Joe turned and strode back into the house. Ellie was dumbfounded. Joe never rowed and walked off. And what was he cross about anyway? She'd wanted him – *expected* him – to share her happiness. Instead he'd just given her a hard time.

She stomped into the tackroom where Luke was putting away Pericles' travelling gear. 'What's up?' he said, seeing her face.

'That's what I'd like to know!' she snapped. She sighed as she saw his surprise. 'Sorry, it's not you. Just Joe being dumb.'

Luke's eyes narrowed shrewdly. 'Let me guess . . . he didn't like you coming to the show with me?'

Ellie shrugged. She might be spitting mad with Joe but she wasn't about to blurt out what they'd just been arguing about.

But Luke didn't need her confirmation. 'He should have stayed here, taken you out. That's the trouble with Joe – he always feels he has to do his duty but it doesn't make him happy. He certainly shouldn't take it out on you.' He looked at her shrewdly. 'You know, he's not right for you, Ellie.'

Ellie blushed hotly. 'I don't know what you're talking about!'

Luke raised his eyebrows and didn't say anything.

Ellie began to put Gabriel's things away. She didn't want to talk about this with Luke. It felt wrong. Her temper was fading now. 'Gabriel's sorted for the night. I'm going to see Spirit.' She reached the door. 'Luke . . .' she hesitated. 'Don't say anything to Joe about all this.'

'Me?' He raised his eyebrows. 'Would I?'

She didn't answer. She knew by now that it was impossible to predict what Luke would do. Giving a little shake of her head, she walked out.

Spirit was in his stable. He looked surprised to be visited at such a late hour, but as always his eyes glowed with love.

Would Luke say anything to Joe? She hoped not. Now her anger had gone, she was beginning to see the situation through Joe's eyes. He must have been worried about her. And even though he'd said they couldn't be more than friends, she knew he *did* like her and he'd probably been jealous of her having a good time with Luke. *Dumb thing*, she thought, with a rush of sympathy. *He knows I don't like Luke in that way.*

Ellie stood with Spirit for a long time before she felt herself starting to fall asleep and reluctantly went inside.

Joe and Luke were both in the kitchen. Luke was eating a slice of toast and reading a magazine. Joe was making coffee. As Ellie came in, Luke glanced between them. Ellie tensed, wondering if he'd said anything. His eyes flicked to hers and he gave the briefest shake of his head, then looked back down at his magazine. She felt a rush of relief. Joe was concentrating on pouring water from the kettle on to the coffee granules in his mug. He wasn't saying anything but his back seemed to bristle. Ellie felt a weariness sink over her. She knew she should make up with him, but it had been a long day and she didn't feel like dealing with this just now.

'Night,' she sighed.

She wasn't sure if she heard one or two replies.

Chapter Ten

Joe avoided Ellie the next morning. While she was helping with the feeds, he filled the water buckets, and when she helped with the haynets he went to start mucking out. As she pushed a wheelbarrow up to the muck heap she saw Luke riding Lucifer, with Len watching. Half keeping an eye on the horse in the menage, Ellie emptied the wheelbarrow. Luke was riding Lucifer in circles, halting by the gate. Ellie hadn't seen the black gelding being ridden for a few days. She paused to watch as Luke rode Lucifer on around the school. Lucifer was going quite well, although he looked far more tense than the first time she'd seen him ridden. Luke cantered him round a few times and then began to circle by the gate again.

'Push him on. Get him going forward!' Len's voice barked out. The gelding was slowing down as he approached the gate. Luke used a stronger leg aid. Lucifer swished his tail and slowed down even more.

'Trot on!' Luke muttered, kicking him.

Lucifer continued past the gate, but as he circled round he started to slow once more as he drew nearer to the gate. Ellie watched closely. Why was he doing that?

'He's messing you around. Get him moving, Luke!' Len called.

Ellie frowned. Lucifer wasn't giving off stubborn, disobedient vibes. If anything, she got the impression he was confused and uncertain.

Luke smacked Lucifer. The gelding's ears flattened and he leapt forward, throwing his head down.

'Let's have none of this. He's playing silly buggers!' Len came striding towards him. 'Make him listen to you, Luke. Show him who's boss. A horse like that will take every advantage he can. Give him a smack!'

Ellie heard Stuart shouting her name on the yard. Hoping that Lucifer would settle down soon, she pushed the wheelbarrow back down the slope.

When Luke came in from riding Lucifer, he looked hot and fed up.

'Did Lucifer get any better?' Ellie asked, joining him in the tackroom.

Luke shook his head. 'He went past the gate in the end, but he was all over the place for the rest of the session. I asked him to go left and he'd go right; I'd want him to go back and he'd go forward. He ended by rearing up. I hope he'll be better tomorrow when

Jeff comes. And it's the first show in a month. I don't know what's up with him. He was so good when he first arrived. He's getting worse each day at the moment and Len's instructions just don't seem to be working.'

Ellie had been thinking about what she'd seen in the menage and she'd had an idea. 'You don't think he was slowing down at the gate because you'd been practising halts there with him, do you? Maybe he was trying to please you – thinking that's what you wanted – and then he got confused when you hit him. He seemed really bewildered.'

Luke frowned. 'Len reckoned he was just throwing his weight around.'

'But he didn't look as if he was.' Ellie wanted to convince Luke. 'Honestly, it didn't seem like that. It really didn't. I think he was trying to please.' She frowned. 'I wonder if joining-up would help him? Maybe Joe could try.'

Luke stared at her as if she was mad. 'Ellie, if you value your life, don't even begin to suggest such a thing to Len.'

'But –'

'No – don't! He's getting wound up enough about Lucifer as it is right now. If you suggest something like that he'll explode. Sure, he lets Joe mess about with the youngsters in the morning, but Lucifer's one of the most important horses on the yard. There's no way he'd let Joe try something like join-up with him.'

Just then, Joe came into the tackroom. Seeing them so deep in intense conversation, he stopped.

'Hi,' said Luke.

'Hi,' Joe muttered, then grabbed a pair of knee boots and left.

Luke raised his eyebrows at Ellie. 'Still not been forgiven then?'

She sighed. 'Nope.'

Luke dumped Lucifer's saddle on the saddle rack. 'You know,' he said, glancing at her, his tone changing. 'The show yesterday was fun.'

Ellie nodded but her thoughts were with Joe. She hated him being in a mood with her. She chewed a fingernail. She wanted to make up but there were always so many other people around. *I'll talk to him as soon as I can*, she decided.

But Ellie's good intentions came to nothing. It was such a busy day that she didn't have a chance to talk to Joe at all. There were horses to get ready for a show the next day and the horsebox needed to be loaded for an early start. In the afternoon, Len tried backing Solo for the first time – or at least the first official time. The chestnut pony behaved faultlessly. He looked slightly surprised to have Len there, but was completely happy to be led round, tacked up and for Joe to sit on his back.

'Looks as if your extra handling's done some good,' Ellie heard Len say to Joe as she watched from the gate. 'But then he's always been an easy pony.'

That evening Ellie hoped to speak to Joe alone, but he stayed downstairs, talking to Len about the show. In the end, Ellie went outside. Lucifer was looking over his door. Ellie remembered how he had been that day and thought of Jeff Hallett coming to see him tomorrow. They really had to get to the bottom of his problems. Ignoring his flattened ears, she let herself into his stable. He shot to the back and stared at her warily. 'It's OK, boy,' Ellie soothed. Lucifer turned his back to her, threatening to kick. His body bristled with tension. *I just want to help*, she told him in her head. *Talk to me.*

She edged closer. When she had spoken to Troy she'd been touching him, she reasoned, but as soon as she was within touching distance Lucifer stamped a back hoof down in his straw bed. Ellie took no notice. She was sure she needed to get close enough to touch him. However, as she tried to get round towards his head and neck, he swung his hindquarters at her threateningly.

'I only want to help you,' she told him in exasperation.

She tried again, but this time Lucifer lashed out with his back hoof.

Ellie paused. She wasn't frightened because she

didn't feel that Lucifer really intended to hurt her. Although he'd been threatening ever since he arrived, he hadn't actually bitten or kicked anyone. And if he'd wanted to hurt Ellie, he could have chased her out of the stable by now. Her instincts told her that Lucifer's behaviour was meant as a warning to keep her away. But if she did that, she couldn't help him. Ignoring his warning, she moved in on his head again. This time he swung round, his teeth snapping at her. She jumped back just in time. Ellie felt like stamping her own foot in the straw. This was pointless. She was getting nowhere and Lucifer was just increasingly wound up.

With a sigh, Ellie gave up and left the stable.

I just don't understand, she told Spirit five minutes later. *He won't speak to me, but why not? I can talk with other horses – I was able to with Troy. What do I need to do, Spirit?*

The grey horse nuzzled her. *Listen carefully.*

A picture grew in her mind – she saw herself and Lucifer. She was just standing there. Ellie caught her breath, waiting for him to show her what to do. But once again nothing happened.

I can't see what you're trying to say, she said in frustration. She sighed, feeling stupid. *I'm sorry.* She patted Spirit. *We can talk again later. I'd better go.*

Spirit was still watching her as she left the stable.

*

Ellie fell into bed exhausted that night. She half woke up at about 5 a.m. as she heard Joe getting up to set off for the show with Stuart and the horses. 'Good luck,' she whispered to him from her bed. Rolling over, she decided that as soon as he was back she'd make sure they talked. She hated there being such an atmosphere between them.

An hour and a half later her alarm clock woke her. She staggered out of bed and, throwing on the first clothes that came to hand, went outside.

'That's what I like about you, Ellie. You always make such an effort in the mornings,' Luke commented as she went into the kitchen.

Looking down, Ellie realized she was wearing an old pink sweatshirt with holes in and there was a stain down the front of her purple jodhpurs. 'I guess I'd better get changed before Jeff Hallett arrives,' she sighed as she made herself a mug of coffee.

Len came in. 'Soon as the breakfasts are done, get that black gelding groomed and ready for Jeff's visit. Make sure he behaves a damn sight better than yesterday. After he's been ridden he can go out in the field with one of the others. It's time he had some company out there.' He rubbed his hands. 'Let's get started!'

By the time Jeff Hallett arrived later that morning, Lucifer was tacked up and ready in his stable. As Luke led him out, Jeff Hallett nodded approvingly.

'He's looking a million dollars.' Ellie had to agree. With his muscles rippling under his satin-soft black coat, Lucifer looked every inch a champion show horse.

'Let's get him into the ring then,' said Len with a nod at Luke.

Ellie followed them. At first Luke rode Lucifer on a long rein and everything was fine. The horse relaxed and walked and trotted round calmly, showing off his beautiful paces.

'He's looking good,' commented Jeff, pleased.

But as Luke gathered up the reins, Ellie sensed a change in Lucifer. Tension prickled in the air around him and he put his head up. Feeling the gelding's pace slow, Luke used his legs strongly. Lucifer swished his tail and pinned back his ears. Conscious of Jeff watching, Luke smacked him and Lucifer exploded. Plunging forward, he threw his head down. Luke kept his seat and pulled the horse's head up, but as he smacked him again Lucifer went wild, kicking his heels up in a series of twisting bucks.

'Christ Almighty!' The exclamation burst out of Jeff.

Len was already through the gate. 'Get him together, Luke!'

Ellie had no idea how Luke managed to stay on top of the horse, but he did, and finally he managed to pull Lucifer into a circle and stop him. Len reached them and grabbed hold of the bridle. Lucifer snorted but stayed still.

'What the hell was all that about?' demanded Jeff Hallett.

'There must be something up with him. He's never done anything like that before. Maybe there's a soreness somewhere,' Len said. 'Off you get, Luke. We'll get the vet and have him checked out.'

Ellie saw a brief look pass between them as Luke dismounted. 'Yeah, he's never behaved like that before,' said Luke to Jeff.

Jeff was frowning. 'He'd better not have done.' He turned to Len. 'I'm paying you good money to make sure that horse is in the ring and gets his ticket for the Horse of the Year. He won't win anything if he behaves like a bucking broncho. He'll embarrass us all.'

'He won't do that. Don't worry.' Len's voice was jovial. 'He's been a dream to work with the last few days. There must be something up with him today. He's a winning horse, there's no doubt about it.'

Jeff Hallett looked slightly mollified. 'Right, well, see you get him sorted. Isn't Anna entered for a show on him soon?'

'Aye, in four weeks' time. We'll have him ready for then,' said Len, his voice ringing with a confidence that Ellie was sure he didn't feel.

'Good.' Jeff Hallett looked at Len as Luke led Lucifer out of the school. 'I brought him here because

I thought you were the best. That's why I sponsor you. And if you're not . . .' His words hung dangerously in the air.

'We are. There's nothing to worry about,' said Len levelly.

'I hope not. I'll see you at the show with him in four weeks' time and I expect him to be in the final line up.' Giving a brief nod, Jeff Hallett strode back to the car park. Len watched him go and then, swearing under his breath, went back to the yard.

Ellie stood by the ring. What had been up with Lucifer? He hadn't gone well the day before but he hadn't tried to buck Luke off like that. Her heart sank as she heard Len shout at Helen about some loose straw on the yard, and then at Sasha for not hanging a headcollar up properly. He'd be in a foul mood all day now. *We'd all better keep out of his way*, she realized, her heart sinking.

However, staying out of her uncle's way was impossible. The disastrous meeting with Jeff had put him in such a dark mood that he seemed determined to pick fault with everyone. Ellie was roared at for using a plastic curry comb on Picasso's tail instead of untangling it knot by knot with her fingers, and when Len checked a water bucket she was refilling and found it hadn't been scrubbed out properly, he threw it across the yard.

Len checked Lucifer over but found nothing wrong with him – no stiffness, no sore patches, nothing. There was no reason why the horse should have behaved as he did.

At lunchtime, Ellie tacked Spirit up. After not riding him the day before, she was determined to today. She had just led him to the courtyard and mounted when she heard Len shouting to Luke. 'Luke! Get Merlin and stick him in the field with Lucifer. We'll see if being out with another horse helps him calm down. I've got John coming this afternoon to have a look at him too.'

Ellie felt a prickle of unease. She hoped Merlin would be all right out with Lucifer. 'Come on, boy,' she said, touching her heels to Spirit's sides. He didn't move. 'Come on.'

He made a whickering nose and shook his head, taking a step backwards.

'What is it?' Ellie clicked her tongue. 'Walk on.'

Spirit pulled up the slope towards the pony barn.

'No, we're going out for a ride.' Ellie was puzzled. She squeezed with her legs again and Spirit walked on. But he moved reluctantly, looking round over his shoulder, and as they reached the car park and rode out on to the lane he lifted his head, stopped dead, and gave a whinny so loud that it shook him. 'What's the matter, boy?' Ellie asked.

She wished she could talk to him properly, but

she'd tried connecting with him before when she was riding and it had never worked. They usually had to be standing still.

Spirit finally walked on but Ellie was left with the uncomfortable feeling that something was wrong. She wasn't sure quite how to define it, he didn't feel nervous or in pain but she could sense a feeling of trepidation in the air around him. Almost as if he was very worried about something.

They reached the end of the lane and crossed over the quiet, winding road into the woods. The banks at the side of the bridle path were covered with bushy plants full of pink flowers; bluebells pushed themselves up in the roots of trees. It was quiet and peaceful with only the sound of birds singing, but Ellie couldn't get rid of the feeling that something was very wrong.

It preyed on her mind, and when she headed for home and saw the vet's car at the other end of the lane she felt a lurch of alarm. But then she remembered that Len had arranged for the vet to check Lucifer out.

Spirit pulled at the reins, wanting to trot. She let him, only trying to slow him down when they neared the car park, but Spirit had no intention of walking calmly. He whinnied twice and Ellie was suddenly gripped with a strange sense of urgency. Jumping off, she led him to the courtyard. The sight that met her eyes made her stop dead. Helen and Sasha were both crying. Luke had his arm round them both.

'What's happened?' Ellie could feel icy pinpricks tingling over her skin. 'What's going on?' She looked from one to the other.

Luke looked up, his eyes for once stunned and without a glint of humour. It was then that Ellie knew it was really bad.

'It's Merlin,' Sasha sobbed. 'It's . . . he's . . .'

'What? He's what? What's happened?' Ellie's voice rose. Spirit nudged her back but for once she ignored him.

'Lucifer attacked him,' said Luke. 'When Merlin was put in the field with him, Lucifer went for him. Merlin tried to get away but Lucifer chased him. We couldn't stop him. In the end Merlin tried to jump the cattle grid to escape.'

'And?' Ellie stared at him.

'He didn't quite make it. He caught his back foot.'

Ellie's heart seemed to stop. 'Has he broken his leg?' A broken leg meant a horse would have to be put down.

'No, but he ripped his tendon to pieces.'

Relief rushed through Ellie. Tendons could mend. She knew that from having been on her dad's vet rounds with him. They needed a lot of rest and they didn't always get better, but often with a year off, the horse or pony would recover. 'So that's why the vet's here?' Luke nodded. 'Oh, poor Merlin.' She looked at the three of them in front of her, not understanding why they were so upset. 'I guess he'll just have to be turned out for a year, but at least he hasn't broken it and –'

'Ellie,' Luke broke in. 'They're going to put him down.'

She blinked, the words not seeming to make sense. 'Put him down?'

Luke nodded and Sasha started to cry more. 'Len won't keep him for a year if he can't work and there's no guarantee he'll get better anyway. He's old, he might not mend.'

Ellie was shaking her head. 'They can't put him down. He's Joe's pony . . .'

She saw Luke's face and knew with absolute certainty that her uncle could do anything he liked. 'No!' she cried. And leaving Spirit where he stood, she sprinted towards the field.

Chapter Eleven

All Ellie's thoughts were fixed on one point: they were going to put Merlin down. She was aware of everything around her – the sound of her boots falling on the gravel, her breath coming in short gasps, the pale blue sky with white clouds scudding across it. She felt like she was running in slow motion. *Merlin, Merlin, Merlin* . . .

The single word pounded over and over in her head.

As she rounded the bend the sight in front of her almost made her throw up. While Lucifer trotted uneasily up and down the line of electric tape, her uncle and John Taylor were standing by Merlin near the cattle grid. The pony's head was low and his left hind leg was lifted off the ground. Even from such a distance, Ellie could feel the waves of pain coming from him. Racing to the gate, she clambered over. Lucifer looked at her and snorted. Ignoring him, she ran up the field, her eyes fixed on the bay pony, each breath hurting her chest now.

She reached them just as John started walking away. 'I'll go and fetch it from the car,' she heard him saying to her uncle.

'What are you doing?' Ellie gasped.

Her uncle looked at her in surprise. 'What's it to you?'

Ellie reached Merlin and touched his neck, for a moment blocking out her uncle, taking in the pony's trembling sides, his heavy breathing, his eyes clouded with pain. She looked at his leg and winced. She'd seen many injured animals when she had helped her dad, and this was bad. Merlin's leg was torn open and blood was running down it. But it didn't have to mean the end. 'It's just his tendon. Luke said.' She looked at her uncle.

'There's no just about it.'

'But all he needs is rest. He might get better.'

'He's old. His time's up.'

Ellie felt as if she was in the worst sort of nightmare, seeing something bad about to happen, being unable to stop it. 'But you can't put him down! If you just left him out in the field, kept him off work . . .'

Her uncle's face was set and closed. 'I'm not a charity.'

'What about Joe?' Ellie's voice rose desperately. 'At least wait until he's back. Merlin's his pony.'

'He'll do what I say and I'm not leaving the pony to suffer more. It's got to be done now. Good lad.' Len patted Merlin and walked off.

'No! You can't!' Ellie shouted. 'You can't do it!' But Len ignored her.

Ellie swung round to the pony, her heart hammering in her chest. She couldn't let this happen. 'It's OK, sweetie. It's all right,' she whispered frantically. The breeze seemed to lift up her futile words and sweep them away. Ellie moved quickly to Merlin's head and took the weight of it in her hands, one on either side of his face. She bent her forehead to his, instinctively pouring love out, not knowing what she was doing but sending everything she could, wishing she could heal him.

Instantly she felt it – the click, the connection. The link she had been looking for so hard with Lucifer. Waves of Merlin's pain rolled over her. It was almost more than she could bear.

It'll be OK, it'll be OK, she told him, her mind racing through possible solutions. Maybe she could get him away from here. But how, with his leg . . .?

She felt his desperate pain and concentrated on that again. The pony's trembling quietened. *Hush now*. Little by little she felt a change in the energy around them, a sense of peace gradually chasing the fear and pain away. She felt as if she and Merlin were cut off from the world. *Love, more love*, her instincts said. She gave it with every cell of her being. *I'm here with you. Don't worry. Don't be scared*, she told him. *You'll be OK. I know you will. I'll think of something. I will. I'll . . .*

She jumped as she heard the sound of footsteps nearby and looked round. John was standing there, the humane killer weighing heavily in his hand. Ellie swallowed. She knew it would send a bolt straight into Merlin's brain and kill him instantly. Suddenly it came crashing down on her that there was nothing she could do to stop this. It was going to happen.

'No,' she whispered, shaking her head hopelessly.

'I have to, love. Your uncle wants me to and it's his pony.'

A hard lump blocked Ellie's throat. 'But Merlin could get better.'

The vet looked at her, his gaze sad. 'Maybe. Maybe not. He wouldn't mend easily at his age.'

Tears started in Ellie's eyes. This wasn't fair. Why couldn't she be older? Why couldn't she stop it? 'Joe's not here,' she said, her voice cracking.

'The lad'll be upset, I know. But we can't let this old boy suffer any more. It's not fair. He won't know a thing about it.' John walked past her and ruffled Merlin's thick mane. 'Come on, my beauty. Let's see you off.'

Tears were running down Ellie's cheeks now, falling on to her coat as she stared down at Merlin's sweet face, his eyes so trusting as he looked up at her. He didn't know what was about to happen.

John's voice cut through the air. 'You'd better move out of the way, Ellie. He'll go down fast.'

She turned away with a sob as the vet moved to where she'd been standing and lifted the gun. Hugging her arms around herself, she tried to think of something to do or say to stop it . . . There was a muffled shot and then a thud. She swung round. The chestnut pony was lying on the ground on his side. His eyes were open but he was dead.

A half cry choked out of her as she flung herself down beside him.

'Come on now.' She felt John pat her shoulder.

Ellie shook her head. She couldn't speak. If she opened her mouth she didn't know what would come out. *No, no, no . . .*

To her relief, the vet seemed to understand. He left her with the pony and walked away. Ellie didn't blame him for a second for what he'd done. She knew vets had to put animals to sleep. No vet ever liked doing it. It wasn't his fault.

But it *was* her uncle's.

Hot tears streamed down her face as she knelt beside Merlin, stroking his neck over and over again. He had been so brave, so willing. He had made so many children happy, given everything all his life and now, in a few seconds, he had gone.

It's not fair!

She saw the photos of him in Joe's room, remembered the smile on Joe's face only the other day as he'd told her how Merlin used to look after him in shows, the trust in Merlin's eyes as he gazed at Joe. His life shouldn't have ended like this. Not after he had given so much, been loved so much . . .

Oh, Joe, she thought as she stroked the bay pony's now lifeless body, feeling no connection, no energy, just a fading warmth. *What are you going to say?*

Ellie stayed with Merlin until the tractor arrived from the local kennels to take him away. She left then. She knew to the men involved that Merlin was just a piece of meat, and she didn't want to see him being hauled on to the trailer, manhandled. It seemed utterly wrong for a pony who had given so much to people all his life. She walked slowly back to the gate, her face stiff with dried tears. Lucifer was grazing now with short unsettled bites. She had never hated an animal in her life, but for an instant she hated him for what he had done.

She breathed out. *No*. Even with the grief still throbbing through her she could sense the unhappiness and fear in him. There was something wrong with him, she was sure of it. She couldn't hate him.

Climbing the gate, she felt numb. The thought of

Joe still at the show, not knowing what had just happened, twisted her up inside. How would he feel when he found out? All thoughts of their argument had gone; it seemed so petty now. *I've got to call him*, she thought.

She went to Spirit's stable. Luke had put him away and untacked him. The grey horse whinnied when he saw her. She leant against him, drawing strength, and then, taking a deep breath, she reached for her phone. Her fingers trembled as she found Joe's mobile number and pressed the call button. The call went straight through to voicemail.

'*Hi, I can't take your call right now. Leave me a message and I'll ring you back.*'

Ellie swallowed as she heard the beep. 'Hi. It's . . . um . . . it's me. Ellie. Look, can you ring me when you get this?' She hesitated, longing to say something more, longing to tell him how much she cared. But what could she say? She clicked the OFF button. Then she texted him: 'Call me PLEASE. E x'

Slipping her phone back in her pocket, she wondered what she'd say when Joe rang. Spirit nudged her and, shutting her eyes, she let herself open up to him, telling him what had happened. *I wanted to stop it. I couldn't. Uncle Len wouldn't listen.*

She felt his sympathy. Words came into her head. *Do not be unhappy. His pain is over.*

But he's dead, Spirit.

Horses walk in the present. Spirit breathed softly on her hands. *Keep your love for the living.*

He sent her a picture of Lucifer in his stable.

Ellie tried to push the image away. She didn't want to think about Lucifer right then. But the picture stayed. Ellie turned away from him, breaking the connection. When she looked back, Spirit was still watching her.

It was the longest afternoon Ellie had ever known. She waited nervously for her phone to ring but it didn't. She wondered if Joe thought she was just phoning him to talk about their quarrel. Maybe he was ignoring her on purpose. *Oh, please ring*, she thought, taking her phone out and double-checking the messages for about the fiftieth time. She wasn't looking forward to the conversation but she hated him not knowing what had happened.

Everyone was quiet on the yard. Helen and Sasha were still upset. Luke kept everyone going, shouldering the burden of all the work and keeping cheerful. Her uncle stayed out of the way. Ellie was glad of that. Whenever she thought about him she wanted to scream and shout at him. How could he have ordered that Merlin be shot like that? He could have saved him. It wouldn't have cost much money to keep him in the field for a year. The pony could have got better. But no. Len's words rang in her ears: *I'm not a charity.*

At six o'clock, after the grooms had left, Stuart finally drove the horsebox into the car park. Ellie watched from the courtyard as they started to unload the ponies. Her feet suddenly felt frozen to the ground. She'd been waiting all afternoon to speak to Joe, but now she couldn't tell him, she just couldn't. She looked at the house but the door stayed closed, her uncle inside.

Ellie didn't think she'd ever felt sicker in her life. She waited by Gabriel's stable, patting him and trying not to look at Lucifer who was tossing his head over his half door. Stuart and Joe unloaded the ponies and came down from the barn, talking.

'Hi,' called Stuart, heading for the tackroom.

Joe gave her a brief smile and followed him. Ellie blinked. After all that had happened, it was hard to remember that Joe and she were still not really speaking. 'Joe!' The word burst out of her. He stopped and looked round.

'Yeah.'

Ellie licked her lips. 'You . . . you didn't answer my messages.'

Joe looked slightly guilty. 'Sorry, I was just busy with the ponies. I thought we could talk when I got back.' He frowned as he read her expression. 'What's up?'

She took a breath. 'Joe, it's Merlin.'

Joe was instantly alarmed. 'What's the matter with him?'

There was no easy way to say it. Ellie's throat felt dry. This was the hardest thing she'd ever had to do. 'He's . . . he's dead.'

She saw the look of incredulity, the frown, the dawning realization that she wasn't joking.

'It happened this afternoon.' The words tumbled desperately out of her. 'He was put out with Lucifer. Lucifer attacked him, he tried to jump the cattle grid and didn't make it. His leg was a mess . . .'

Joe stared at her. 'He's dead?'

'Yes, John came. Your dad . . .' She swallowed again. 'Your dad told him to put Merlin down.'

Joe started to shake his head.

She didn't know what to say. Sorry was too small a word. She wished she could hug him, somehow make him feel better, but he was already turning. He marched towards the house. Then abruptly he changed direction and hurried up to the barn.

Ellie went after him. As she passed the house, the door opened and Len looked out, slippers on his feet. 'Is he back then?'

Ellie didn't answer as she raced after Joe.

Chapter Twelve

Joe stood in the barn, staring at Merlin's empty stable. The bed was still as the pony had left it that morning, the night rug slung over the door, the haynet half-eaten.

Ellie approached him cautiously. 'Joe?'

Joe didn't look round. 'He's really dead?'

'Yes.' Ellie reached his side.

'What happened?' Joe touched the pony's rug, as if trying to make it real by touching, feeling. His voice was tight. 'Tell me it all.'

Ellie told him again, filling in the details, tears threatening to spill down her cheeks again as she relived the moment. She struggled to control herself.

'And it was Dad who said to shoot him . . .' Ellie could tell Joe was struggling to hold in his feelings.

Ellie nodded.

There was the sound of the barn door opening. It was Len and Luke. Ellie glanced at Joe, expecting an explosion, but he just turned swiftly away.

'So you've heard?' Len said.

Joe nodded.

'It had to be done.' Len's voice was brusque. 'The pony was in pain.'

Ellie could almost see the tension sparking around Joe but he didn't speak.

'Well?' said Len at last.

'Well, what?' Joe ground out.

'Aren't you going to say something more? If you don't like what I did, lad, why don't you say it? Tell me about it.' Ellie saw the challenge in her uncle's eyes.

'What good would it do?'

Len's gaze narrowed scornfully. 'Aren't you going to show some guts for once in your life?'

'Guts!' Joe finally lost it and swung round furiously. 'That's all you think about, isn't it? You think it shows guts if someone shouts and yells, if they hit people, if they beat a horse up to make it do what they want, if they'll get into a fight. You make me sick!'

Len had folded his arms as Joe shouted. Ellie could see a faint look of satisfaction in his eyes. *He's glad Joe's yelling at him*, she realized, feeling horrified. 'That's it. Come on, lad,' Len urged, his voice goading. 'You tell me what you really think of me now.'

'OK, I'll tell you what I really think! There's nothing inside you. People don't matter to you. Horses only matter if they win. You get a kick from bullying.

That's why Mum left you and you hate me because I remind you of her!' His dad squared up as if about to fight but Joe didn't move away. He stepped closer to his dad, his eyes blazing. 'You're a –'

'Joe!' Luke swiftly stepped in front of him. 'Stop it,' he said in a low voice.

'Leave him,' ordered Len. 'If he wants to have a go at me, let him.'

Luke ignored him, his attention on his cousin's angry face. 'Joe!'

Joe drew in a deep breath. 'No, I'm not going to be like you.' He turned abruptly. 'I'm going out. Will you give me a ride into town, Luke?'

'Sure,' said Luke. 'Get the spare helmet.'

Joe strode down the aisle towards the door.

'So that's it, is it?' Len shouted. 'Running away now, are you? I might have known. You flamin' coward!' He spat the word out. His voice was cut off by the slam of the barn door.

Len turned to Luke. 'And what do you think *you're* doing – interfering, taking sides?'

Luke shrugged coolly. 'He's got a right to be upset, Len. Even you can see that.'

They faced up to each other for a moment and then Len grunted. 'He's too damn soft about the ponies.'

Luke's eyes met Ellie's briefly, then he turned and followed Joe.

It was just Ellie and Len in the barn.

'I hate you,' she said, her voice shaking.

He gave a dry laugh. 'Tough that you're bloody stuck with me then until you're eighteen.' With that he turned and walked away. Ellie watched him go and then buried her face in Merlin's rug and cried.

Ellie didn't want to go into the house that night so she sought refuge in Spirit's stable. She groomed him, losing herself in the rhythmic sweep of the body brush over his coat and on to the curry comb. At last, exhausted, she rugged him up and sank down in a pile of clean straw by his manger. When would Joe and Luke be back? She shut her eyes, trying to block out the images of the day.

She must have drifted off to sleep because some time later she heard a motorbike. She was instantly awake and got to her feet. Letting herself out of the stable, she ran to the car park just in time to meet Luke coming up the slope, his helmet under his arm.

'Where's Joe?'

'Didn't want to come home.' Luke looked tired for once and ran a hand through his hair. 'I tried to persuade him but he wanted to be on his own.'

'But how will he get back?'

'I dunno. Taxi. I'm not his keeper.'

'You shouldn't have left him there!' Worry made her snap.

'What could I do? Drag him home? He wanted to be on his own, Ellie.' Luke gave a brief shake of his head. 'I'm going in.'

Ellie watched him go, then headed back to Spirit's stall. The horse snorted as she came in, and she sank down on the straw again. Leaning her head against the stable wall, she shut her eyes. There was the sound of hooves moving in the straw and she felt warm breath on her hands. Opening her eyes, she looked into Spirit's face. He was there for her – always there. She touched his cheek, stroking it gently until she fell asleep.

Ellie didn't know what woke her, but when she blinked her eyes open she wondered for a moment where she was. All she could see was wooden walls and her body felt stiff and cold, her neck aching. As she saw Spirit lying down in the straw just in front of her it all came flooding back. *Merlin. Joe . . .*

Checking her watch, she saw that it was six o'clock in the morning. The sky outside was just getting light. She staggered to her feet. Was Joe back? Straw was sticking to her hair and clothes. Rubbing her face, she went to the door. She should go in and check.

As she walked up to the house, she glanced down the lane. A figure was walking along, barely visible in the half-light. But she knew instantly it was Joe. Changing direction, she ran to meet him.

'Joe!'

He looked at her in surprise. 'What are you doing up?' His face was pale, deep purple shadows under his eyes, his hair tousled into spikes.

'I didn't want to go inside. I've been waiting for you to come home.'

'You daft thing.' He managed a small smile.

'Where have you been?' Ellie demanded.

'Just walking. When Luke left I wandered round for a bit and then decided to walk home.' He gave a short laugh. 'I suppose I went the long way.'

'You shouldn't have been walking by yourself in the dark. You could have got run over or lost or anything.'

'So? Who'd have cared?'

'Me!' She looked at him. 'Of course me.'

She saw the grief in his face then. 'Oh, Joe.' Stepping forward, she flung her arms round his neck and hugged him tightly, everything else fading. None of the stuff they'd been arguing about mattered now. She just wanted to take away the pain and make him better.

He buried his head in her hair, a sob breaking through him. 'I can't bear it, Ellie.'

'I know. I do. I really do know.' Words tumbled through her mind: *it'll be all right . . . don't worry . . . you'll get over it . . .*

She wanted to say them, to try and comfort him, but she knew how little effect such words had. A picture of Spirit came into her head and she remembered the times she'd cried into his mane and the way he had let her do that. Not offering opinions in the way humans did, but just comforting her by being there. She bit her tongue and held the words in.

Joe looked at her. 'Was anyone with him when he died?'

'Me. I wanted to stop it, but when I couldn't I stayed with him until it was over. And afterwards.' Ellie shut her eyes, trying to block out the picture of the tractor chugging over the field. She was glad Joe had been spared that.

Joe stepped back.

'What are you going to do?' Ellie asked him.

'Do?' He looked taken aback. 'What *can* I do?'

'Well, are you going to say something more to your dad?'

'What's the point?' Joe looked defeated, his earlier fighting mood completely gone. 'Nothing will change him, and it won't bring Merlin back.' He swallowed. 'I suppose I'd better go in, take a shower and get ready for the show.'

Ellie stared. 'You're not seriously thinking of going to the show today?'

'The ponies are entered. I just have to get on with life.'

'But, Joe –'

He shrugged. 'It's better this way.'

He started walking towards the farm. Ellie fell into step beside him. 'You can't just keep quiet – you can't carry on as if nothing's happened!'

'Ellie. Dad is Dad and life is life. It's what I'm stuck with. There's no point fighting it.'

'No point? That's stupid! You can't think like that! Joe, you don't always have to do what your dad or everyone else wants! You *can* fight things!'

But Joe carried on walking. 'Let's just go in,' he said wearily.

She followed him into the kitchen, unable to believe that he planned to go to the show as if it was a normal day. They were taking their boots and coats off when Len came downstairs in his dressing gown. 'Oh, it's you two. You've finally come in, have you?' He looked at Ellie. 'Luke said you were asleep in the stable.'

Ellie realized that meant Luke had come looking for her. But she didn't have time to wonder about it; she just gave a brief nod. Joe might not want a scene, but she couldn't forgive that easily.

'And *you've* got over your temper tantrum, have you?' Len said, looking at Joe.

Ellie stiffened on Joe's behalf. Joe put a hand quickly on her arm.

'What time are we leaving for the show?' he asked Len coolly.

'Seven o'clock.' Len sniffed. 'You'd better clean yourself up and get those ponies ready.'

Joe headed upstairs without a word.

Ellie gave Len a furious look.

Joe paused. 'Ellie. Come on.'

Ellie hesitated, but the plea in his voice was unmistakable and the last thing she wanted was to increase his misery. She swung round and followed him. 'You should have said something,' she said in frustration.

Joe stopped on the landing, ignoring her words. 'Will you give me a hand getting the ponies ready?'

She saw the utter weariness in his face. 'Of course,' she sighed. 'I'll just change my clothes, then I'll be straight down.'

As Len and Joe left for the show, her uncle barked an order at Luke: 'Get that black gelding going well today. There's less than four weeks until his first show. Make sure he knows who's boss.'

'Will do.' Ellie heard the tension in Luke's voice. She wondered if he still thought Len was a better father than his own.

Luke took Lucifer into the school but the horse was even more resistant than the day before, shaking his head, swishing his tail and threatening to rear. Ellie was pleased to see him playing up. She hoped her uncle wouldn't be able to get Lucifer going properly, so Jeff Hallett would take his horse and maybe even his sponsorship away.

It would serve him right, she thought fiercely as she fetched Spirit's bridle for a ride at lunchtime.

As they left the yard and headed up to the hills she felt the tension she'd been holding inside her release. It had been such a difficult twenty-four hours. Focusing on the small things she saw around her – the bits of wool caught in the barbed-wire fence; the stones on the path that had fallen out of a wall; thinking of Spirit with his stride swinging out beneath her – Ellie felt everything else fade to the back of her mind.

When the land levelled out, she stopped Spirit and looked down over the valley. The yard was beneath her, with other grey stone farms dotted around the slopes, and further down in the valley was the town. Ellie wondered where Joe was. Leaning forward, she put her arms round Spirit's neck.

Poor Joe. He'd be kept busy at the show, but she knew only too well that being busy just kept grief at bay for a while; it didn't make it go away.

She rested her head against Spirit's mane. *Oh, Spirit*, she thought. *Why is life so hard sometimes?*

Love came from him but there was no answer to her question.

I guess horses don't think like that, she thought wistfully. *They don't think why me, or wonder why everything is so hard*. Never, in all the times Spirit had spoken to her about his own past, had she felt a complaint or a sense of unfairness. She remembered what Spirit had told her about horses the night before: *Horses walk in the present.*

It was true. Horses got on with things. They rarely wasted time by questioning why, or wondering if things could be different. They existed in the moment.

Horses are incredible, Ellie told Spirit.

Different, came the swift reply. She saw a picture of herself cradling Merlin's head: the pony's eyes were closed but there was a real sense of him being comforted. It almost made her want to cry.

I wanted to stop it, she told Spirit.

I know. You couldn't, but you helped. And you can help others too, the ones who are still here.

He sent her a picture of Lucifer in the stable again, just as he had the day before. *He didn't mean it to end as it did. He has problems. He needs someone to understand.*

Ellie hesitated. She didn't want to go anywhere near Lucifer after what he'd done.

Spirit watched her.

With a sigh, she checked her watch. She should get moving. Straightening up, she touched her heels to his sides and they carried on.

When Joe returned from the show, there were two rosettes stuck inside the windscreen of the lorry and her uncle seemed happy. Ellie helped unload the ponies.

'So how was it?' she said, going to find Joe when

she'd settled the ponies in their stables. He was fastening the breast strap on Bill's rug.

'It was a show.' Joe shrugged. 'We won one class, took a fifth in the other. Dad's pleased.'

Rubbing a hand over his eyes, he came out of the stable. He looked utterly drained.

'And how are you feeling?' she asked.

'I don't want to talk about it.'

'OK.' She helped him put the travelling boots and rugs away. If he didn't want to talk that was fine. She wouldn't force him. She remembered her own horror at seeing a bereavement counsellor who'd wanted her to talk about her parents' death, and at the way her friends' parents had tried to make her speak about it. She knew that part of the comfort Spirit gave her was that he never expected her to talk if she didn't feel like it, and he never told her how she should be thinking or feeling. Ever since he'd come into her life he had always just been there for her, whenever she needed, *however* she needed. Joe didn't have a horse like Spirit. But he did have her. In that instant, she promised herself she would be there for him in the same way.

'You look exhausted,' she said as they finished off. 'Come on. No homework tonight. You're going to watch television with me.'

Joe didn't have the strength to argue. He managed a sad smile and they went into the house together.

Chapter Thirteen

Over the next week, Ellie stayed true to her promise. She was there for Joe in any way she could be. He never spoke about Merlin and what had happened, but at times she would catch him looking at Merlin's old stable and see the loss in his eyes. Ellie felt concerned about him. He was withdrawn and quiet, going about his day-to-day life with a deep unhappiness hanging over him. She knew that under the surface he was still angry with his dad, but he kept it all inside. She wished he would say something more to Len, deal with it, but that wasn't his way.

It was probably a good thing. Len was in a black mood. Lucifer's behaviour had grown worse than ever. Len continued with his view that he was a dominant horse, but the more Luke hit him, the more Lucifer fought back, and when Luke tried to ride him with spurs Lucifer had another wild bucking fit. It seemed impossible that he'd be ready for Anna to enter in the show in three weeks' time.

Ellie was glad her uncle was stressed and worried, but when she voiced this to Joe he shook his head.

'This isn't just about Dad, Ellie. If we lose the Equi-Glow sponsorship it could be really bad for us all. Jeff Hallett is generous and gives Dad a lot of money. If we didn't have it, we'd have to sell some of the horses. We couldn't keep nearly as many.' He frowned. 'And it's not good for Lucifer either. He's so unhappy. You can see it written all over him. I wish I could do something. I thought about joining-up with him – it might help – but I know Dad wouldn't even let me try.'

'I wish he'd let you. I bet it would make a difference.' She thought of suggesting they did it in secret, maybe when Len was out, but just looking at Joe's face she knew he wouldn't even consider it. Ellie frowned as she realized that Joe hadn't actually worked with any young horses since Merlin had died, yet it was one of the things that had always made him happiest.

'You might not be able to join-up with Lucifer, but isn't your dad thinking of backing Minstrel soon? Are you going to join-up with him?'

Joe shook his head. 'I'm not in the mood at the moment.'

'But it helped Solo so much.'

'I don't want to.'

Ellie hesitated. She knew that whenever she'd been feeling down about her mum and dad, then helping

Spirit and listening to him had always left her feeling calmer and somehow soothed. 'I think you should.'

'No, Ellie –'

'Please, Joe. Join-up with Minstrel.'

He didn't say anything.

Ellie grabbed the chance. Joe might not feel like doing it, but she was sure it would help him. 'Why don't you do it tomorrow morning? I'll meet you at the barn . . .'

'No,' he started to say.

'Yes. If you're not there, I'll come and drag you out of bed. You're going to join-up with Minstrel. He needs it – and so do you.'

Joe looked as if he would argue, but at the sight of her determined face he gave in. 'OK, OK, anything to keep the peace,' he said, spreading his hands. 'I'll join-up with him.'

'Brilliant!' Ellie beamed.

Joe sighed.

The next morning, at 6 a.m., Ellie met Joe by Minstrel's stall. Minstrel was a three-year-old dark bay thoroughbred that Len hoped to eventually show in the hack classes. Beautiful but highly strung, he was very different from easy-going Solo. As Joe led him down to the ring, with Ellie carrying the saddle, Minstrel peered around, jumping as he saw ghosts in every clump of grass.

'Minstrel!' Joe exclaimed in irritation as the horse shied and knocked into him. He pulled the leadrope hard. 'Stop it!'

Ellie felt a flicker of worry. Joe was usually so patient with horses. She could tell he didn't want to be here. Was she doing the right thing in making him try this? *Yes*. She clung to the instinct that had made her get Joe out with a young horse again.

When they reached the ring Joe took off Minstrel's headcollar and set him free. Minstrel shied away, sending sand over Joe, and cantered to the far fence. Stopping at the last moment, he tossed his head, wheeled round and raced away.

Joe sighed and then, bracing his shoulders, began walking into the centre.

'Good luck,' Ellie called.

Joe didn't look round or reply.

I'm doing the right thing, she told herself. But she couldn't help feeling uneasy.

Minstrel swerved round Joe and stopped dead at the fence again. Joe walked towards him, lifting his arms to send the horse on round the outside of the ring. Minstrel bucked, his back legs kicking out. Ellie saw Joe take a step back, his eyes widening, almost as if he had suddenly realized where he was. Minstrel plunged one way, cantered a few paces, then swung round and galloped straight at Joe.

'Whoa!' Joe jumped back in surprise as Minstrel

thundered past, kicking his legs up with a squeal.

Suddenly Joe had no choice but to concentrate on the horse. Before Ellie's eyes, the reluctance dropped away from him, an intent expression on his face, as he focused on the bay gelding. 'Go on!' he urged, heading after him.

Minstrel made to stop at the fence again, but Joe growled and ran at him, lifting his arms to encourage the horse on. He had to get Minstrel moving round the outside of the ring, not simply going wherever he wanted. With a toss of his head, Minstrel set off at a canter. Joe instinctively positioned himself so that he was level with the horse's hindquarters, sending him on by staying square to the horse, lifting his arms and keeping his eyes locked on to the horse's eyes. Ellie could see that all thoughts of Merlin and his dad had faded away; the only thing on his mind now was how best to work with the horse.

He had to keep Minstrel cantering until the horse showed signs that he wanted come in and be close to him instead of staying away. The skill with join-up was to watch for those signs and respond immediately, letting the horse know that when he wanted to be friends the human in the middle was ready and waiting.

Minstrel tried to stop and swing round again, but Joe was there at his hindquarters, urging him on, making him do what Joe wanted. Minstrel cantered on until Joe blocked his movement by changing his position so he was walking towards the horse's head. Then Minstrel stopped and turned. Ellie saw Joe give a small nod and smile; it was what he had wanted. He was encouraging the horse to listen to him, to react to his body language.

Ellie gradually let out the breath she'd been holding. Joe was working with the horse, really working with him. Minstrel wasn't easy at all. Joe had to concentrate for every second, but eventually the bay gelding's wild canter slowed to a steady pace and then, as Joe eased off the pressure slightly by moving further away, dropped to a trot.

Joe asked the horse to change direction several times, and little by little the horse began to show signs he'd had enough of moving round, that he wanted to come in and be friends with Joe. First his head started to lower and then his inside ear seemed to fix on Joe. His head dropped lower still until his muzzle was almost on the floor and he started to lick and chew.

'Now!' Ellie breathed.

Joe acted at the same moment. Turning away and dropping eye contact, he made his body language non-aggressive. Ellie could see that although he wasn't looking directly at the horse, he was keeping an eye on him. Minstrel slowed to a stop and looked at Joe. Ellie waited for him to come in and join-up, but with a toss of his head Minstrel started walking towards the gate. But Joe wasn't fazed and responded instantly. Turning round, he moved quickly towards the horse, raising his arms. Minstrel set off at a canter again, his eyes surprised.

It only took a couple of circuits before he was slowing down again to a trot and then asking to be friends. This time, when Joe turned away, Minstrel barely hesitated. He slowed to a walk and turned in, coming straight to Joe and halting by his shoulder.

Ellie saw the smile spread across Joe's face as he began to stroke the horse and rub his neck. She saw that he was speaking to him, smiling, totally caught up in what he was doing.

Relief flowed through her. He'd done it. He'd joined-up with Minstrel. She was sure it would help him. She knew how losing herself in talking to Spirit had been like a break from real life, an escape that wasn't possible any other way, not even in sleep. As Joe walked round the ring with Minstrel following him, she could see he wasn't thinking about anything else, just the horse and how best to work with him. He stopped, rubbed the horse's neck and sent him out again. Within a few circuits Minstrel was asking to join-up. This time, when they met in the middle, Joe walked over to the gate.

'Can I have the headcollar and saddle?'

Ellie nodded and climbed over the gate with it.

Joe slipped on Minstrel's headcollar and then saddled him up, as gently and carefully as the first time he'd tried this with Solo. Minstrel turned his head and tried to nibble the saddle flaps, but he didn't look afraid. Joe fastened the girth loosely and then led him round. They returned to the gate with Minstrel walking quietly beside Joe.

'You did it!' Ellie said.

Joe nodded slowly and, for the first time since Merlin had died, Ellie saw a light in his eyes. 'I didn't think I was going to. He was harder than Solo.'

'But you did it,' Ellie told him.

'Yeah.' Joe looked at her. 'Thanks for making me.'

She smiled. 'Any time.'

For a moment she thought he was about to say something else, but he just patted Minstrel's neck and took the saddle off again. 'Let's take him in.'

They led Minstrel up to his stall in an easy silence. Joe took his headcollar off and they stood in the stall together, watching as Minstrel had a drink. 'Will you do some more with him tomorrow?' Ellie asked.

Joe nodded. 'You were right. I should have been working with the horses. It helps.' He looked at her. 'You know that, though, don't you?'

'Yes,' she admitted.

He reached impulsively for her hand. 'Thank you. For everything. I don't how I'd have got through the last week without you. You've been brilliant.'

Ellie didn't know what to say. She blushed.

His fingers tightened on hers and their eyes met.

Suddenly she couldn't help herself. She was swept away by the closeness of the moment and by everything she wanted – everything she was sure he wanted too. 'Joe,' she whispered. 'Nothing else matters apart from us. Please, can't you see that?'

He hesitated and then he pulled her into his arms.

Ellie's breath caught in her throat. This was it! The moment she'd been waiting for.

But as his lips moved down to meet hers, she looked into his eyes and felt as if she'd just been thumped in the stomach. She instantly pulled away.

'What?' Joe said in surprise.

Her eyes searched his. She saw his confusion but beyond that something else – worry, anxiety. She swallowed. 'Why were you about to kiss me just then?'

'Why?' Joe's frown deepened. 'Because you wanted me to.'

His words crashed into her. 'Because *I* wanted you to,' she echoed.

'You do, don't you?' he went on, still frowning. 'I thought this was what you wanted.'

Biting her lip, she took a breath. 'Do you want this too?'

He stared at her, taken aback. 'What? Of course I do!'

She desperately wanted to believe him but her senses were on red alert. 'Really?'

He hesitated.

'Joe!'

'I do want to . . .' His voice trailed off.

She said the word for him. '*But . . .*'

'But . . . but I can't stop thinking about everything else.' He looked completely torn. 'I can't just ignore everything else the way you can, Ellie. I wish I could be like you – as certain as you. I really do. Part of me wants to be so much more than just friends. But I just can't . . .'

Ellie nodded slowly.

'Oh, Ellie,' he groaned, seeing her face. 'I'm sorry. Look, I can forget everything else. I'll try . . .' He reached for her hands again.

'No! We can't do this unless you really want to. It has to make you happy too. Properly happy.'

She waited, desperate for him to tell her it would, but he didn't. And in the silence, she faced the truth. Although she'd dreamt about this, wanted it so much, it couldn't happen.

'Ellie?' he said hesitantly.

She drew in a deep breath, suddenly knowing what she had to do. 'You know,' she said, swallowing, 'I think this a bad idea.'

He looked surprised. 'Really?'

'Yeah.' She nodded and met his gaze. It was one

of the hardest things she'd ever done. 'You're right, Joe. There are way too many problems. It would be just too difficult.'

The relief that flashed across his face stabbed her like a javelin.

'Are you sure about this? Cos maybe we can try . . .'

'No,' she interrupted quickly. 'No trying. Let's just be friends.'

He squeezed her hands. 'The best of friends, Els. Always closer than close.'

She forced a smile, and turned before he could see how upset she was. 'I'll just see Spirit before morning feeds,' she managed to say.

He nodded. 'I'll put the tack away.'

As Ellie turned towards Spirit's stable she broke into a run. Spirit was waiting, looking over his stable door, as if he had sensed she was coming. He whinnied when he saw her.

Ellie fumbled with his door. Getting into the stable, she flung her arms round his neck. All the dreams she'd had about her and Joe crumbled. *It's not going to happen*, she thought. *Not any of it. Not ever.* She pictured his smiling greeny-grey eyes and her heart twisted violently. Joe would never be anything more than a friend. She began to cry.

Spirit breathed softly on her face.

I'm here, he seemed to say. *Everything will be all right.*

Gradually, the storm passed and the tears began to dry on Ellie's face. She felt strangely empty, as if there had once been a landscape of possibilities inside her but now it had been razed to the ground, leaving just dust.

She wanted to hide away but knew she had to be strong. Joe's words echoed in her head: *We'll be the best of friends*. She knew he needed a best friend right then – he was still grieving for Merlin, still desperately unhappy. However much she was hurting, she couldn't make him feel worse.

She drew in a deep breath and promised herself that she would still be there for him. No matter what. Spirit nuzzled her. Stroking his neck, she blinked back the fresh tears that prickled in her eyes.

Chapter Fourteen

Ellie kept her promise. It was hard, but she hid her unhappiness and acted as normally as she could around Joe. It both helped and hurt that he seemed happier – working with Minstrel each morning was easing his grief in the way she'd thought it would. And he seemed happier now that everything had been sorted between the two of them. If anything, he was more relaxed and affectionate with her, even closer, as if before he'd been holding back so she didn't get the wrong idea. Ellie tried to smile and be relaxed back but she found it tough.

She avoided everyone as much as she could, spending every spare moment with Spirit, just being with him, talking to him and grooming him. She found his loving presence so comforting. On Saturday morning she was with him in his stable when he sent her a picture of Lucifer.

Ellie blushed guiltily. She'd been so caught up with Joe that she hadn't tried to talk to Lucifer again, and she knew the horse's behaviour had worsened further. It was his first show in two weeks and, from the conversations she'd overheard, Ellie knew Luke and her uncle were seriously worried. Her uncle had been to a show that day with Joe and some of the horses, leaving firm instructions with Luke to work Lucifer until he was going well – even if it took all day. As she'd been on her way to Spirit's stable she'd passed Luke leading Lucifer up to the menage.

Now Spirit sent her a picture of the black gelding again. *He needs you.*

I've tried talking to him, though, Ellie replied. *And it's never worked.* She didn't want to talk to Lucifer, not after what he had done.

You need to listen.

I do, but he never talks.

No. Listen, Spirit repeated patiently.

Ellie didn't know what he meant. A picture of Joe formed in her head. Her confusion deepened. *Joe? What's Joe got to do with Lucifer?*

The picture got sharper.

Ellie frowned. After making such a mistake with the nettles she was determined not to ignore anything Spirit said, but what did he mean by showing her Joe? *Are you saying I should get Joe to talk to Lucifer?* she thought uncertainly.

No.

Another picture came into her head, this time of

Troy, and then a picture of Merlin as she had tried to comfort him before he'd been put down. Joe, Troy, Merlin . . .

Ellie felt completely confused. What did Spirit mean? From the way they kept alternating in her mind, she was sure he was trying to tell her there was a link between them all. But what was it? She thought hard. *I guess I helped Troy, Joe too, and I did all I could to help and comfort Merlin even though I wasn't able to save him.*

A clump of nettles came into her head again. It was as though she was in Spirit's head, experiencing his feelings. She could feel the need for them. It was coursing through her, deeper than thought, completely instinctive . . .

Instinctive. Ellie slowly drew in her breath as things started clicking into place. Of course! The times she'd helped Troy, Joe and Merlin, she'd simply gone with what her instincts were saying, but with Lucifer . . .

'I haven't been,' she whispered. Her eyes widened as she thought back. Over and over again she had sensed that Lucifer wanted to be left alone and yet what had she done? She'd gone closer to him, tried to touch him. Time after time he'd used his body language to tell her to back off, but she'd been so caught up in doing what had worked with Troy that she'd ignored what Lucifer was telling her. How could she have been so stupid? No wonder he hadn't wanted to connect with her. She'd read enough books on working with horses and seen Joe working with the youngsters enough times. She knew that one of the basic rules to get a horse's trust involved proving that you could listen to them – and that meant responding to their signals. She hadn't done that!

She remembered how she had once thought that she didn't need horse-whispering techniques to help horses, because she could actually talk to them. Well, that only worked if they would speak to her and they wouldn't do that unless they trusted her.

'*That's* why you've been telling me to listen,' she breathed to Spirit. 'I thought you meant I should listen when Lucifer talked to me, but you were telling me I should listen to him *before* he talked – that I should listen to what my instincts were telling me. That I needed to do that if I wanted him to talk.'

He snorted. She shook her head. The pictures he had sent to her suddenly made sense, the pictures showing her standing a little way off from Lucifer, doing nothing. She had thought she hadn't been getting the message clearly, that she wasn't understanding what she needed to do. But the truth was he'd been telling her that all she needed to do was simply watch, listen, respond and wait.

She was overcome with a wave of remorse. All this time she could have been helping Lucifer if she hadn't been so carried away by what she thought she *had* to do. She'd let him go on being unhappy because she hadn't moved on from the way she spoke to Troy. But they were such different horses. Troy loved people. He had sought out her touch and been keen to link minds. Lucifer was wary and reserved. Picasso too, she realized, as she remembered her difficulty talking to him when she'd tried a month ago. She could have kicked herself. She wouldn't dream of riding every horse in the same way, so why had she thought that one approach would work when talking to them?

'I've been so dumb,' she said to Spirit. 'I ignored everything I know.'

Only because you wanted to help so much. There was no blame, just love. *You're learning still.*

I should have learnt faster.

Mistakes happen. She felt a blanket of calm wrap around her and pictures of Troy, Merlin, Joe and Picasso flowed into her mind. She knew what he was saying: be happy for the ways in which she had helped.

A lump suddenly formed in her throat. Whatever she did, Spirit only ever looked for the good.

I'll try again with Lucifer, she told him. *As soon as I can.*

She felt Spirit start to send her a wave of encouragement, then suddenly he tensed, his head lifting.

Keyed into his emotions, Ellie instantly frowned. 'What's the matter?'

A single word jumped straight into her head from him. *Go!*

Ellie blinked. *Go where?*

To Lucifer.

Lucifer? Fear gripped Ellie as she stared at Spirit. *What's happening?*

He needs you now.

Ellie's heart turned a somersault as she remembered seeing Lucifer in the menage with Luke. What was happening? Not stopping to ask more questions, she turned and ran.

As Ellie ran up the slope to the menage she saw Lucifer plunging around wildly, fighting for his head, ears pinned back. Luke was sticking like glue to the saddle. 'Oh no, you don't, you bloody thing!' He brought his whip down on the horse's hindquarters with a loud smacking noise.

'Luke, don't!' Ellie shouted.

Maddened, Lucifer reared up. Luke threw his weight forward.

'Luke!'

But Luke wasn't listening; he brought his whip down again. With a squeal, Lucifer wrenched his head free from Luke's restraining hands and bucked over and over again, great twisting bucks that even

Luke with all his skill couldn't sit on. On the third buck Luke fell forward on to the horse's neck. The fourth sent him crashing to the floor. He hung on to the reins but, with a squeal, Lucifer pulled back, wheeled round and galloped straight at the fence.

'No!' gasped Ellie as Lucifer gathered himself and soared over the top pole, reins flapping and stirrups banging against his sides. He set off up the hillside at a gallop.

'Stupid horse!' Luke yelled, scrambling to his feet unhurt. 'Come back!'

'Yeah, like that's going to work!' shouted Ellie, fear for Lucifer racing through her. If his leg caught in the reins he'd crash down and maybe break a leg. Or what if he got on to a road? 'How could you be such an idiot?' She swung round to Luke, eyes blazing. 'Why did you hit him like that? Now look what you've done. Anything could happen to him –' She broke off, realizing there was no time for blame. They needed to act – and fast. They had to get Lucifer back. Her mind turned to action. 'Look,' she said decisively. 'I'll go after him on Spirit. You take your motorbike.'

Luke's mind was already on the same tracks. 'Yeah, I'll go on to the road and if he comes through the trees, I'll head him off.'

Ellie turned and ran back down the slope.

'What's going on?' demanded Stuart as she grabbed Spirit's bridle from the tackroom.

'Lucifer's jumped the fence and gone into the woods. Ask Luke!'

Spirit was still waiting anxiously by the gate. Ellie threw his bridle on. 'Come on, boy!' she said, vaulting on his back.

A few minutes later, they were cantering away from the yard through the woods. The track led upwards. The trees were thick in this bit of the wood, which Ellie hoped would work to her advantage because it meant Lucifer would probably have stayed on the path. There was no sign of the black gelding, though.

What if something happens to him? she thought frantically, desperately trying not to think about what had happened to Merlin when he was hurt. 'Come on, Spirit.' Clinging to his mane, she urged him on faster. He responded eagerly, mud splashing up around him.

After a few minutes, the track forked into two. Spirit came to a halt. *Which way?* Ellie felt sick. It was impossible to tell which way Lucifer had gone. The ground was churned up in both directions. There were no stray black tail hairs or useful clues. Whatever should she do?

Oh help, Spirit, help, she thought, sitting back in dismay.

Spirit snorted, then set off resolutely down the right-hand track, breaking into a canter within a few strides. Ellie grabbed his mane to stop herself falling off. 'You think it's this way?' She ducked to avoid a branch. Spirit speeded up, swerving round a corner, almost catching Ellie's leg on a tree.

'Steady, boy!' But she was relieved the track they were on led up the mountain and not down to the road.

Digging her knees into his side, she hung on like a limpet as Spirit raced up the hill. Three times Spirit chose the direction they should go in and then suddenly, as they climbed higher and the path became even narrower, he stopped. She clicked her tongue and nudged him with her heels. 'Come on, Spirit!'

But Spirit refused to move. He pawed the ground.

Ellie hesitated. The path seemed completely clear. What was he telling her? Fighting the deep-rooted instincts pushing her forward to find Lucifer, she shut her eyes, took a few calm breaths and tried to connect with Spirit.

As her mind opened, Spirit sent a picture of the black gelding. She had a strong feeling that he was close and saw herself walking on up the track alone.

You want me to go on?

Yes.

But not with you?

She saw a picture of Lucifer and felt waves of antagonism coming from him. She realized what Spirit was telling her. For whatever reason, Lucifer hated other horses, and as long as she was with Spirit she didn't have a chance of getting close to him.

Slipping off Spirit's back, she hesitated. It felt wrong just leaving him. But after everything that had happened she knew she had to listen to him.

Go. I'll wait. You can find him. You have the ability.

Putting her trust in him, Ellie continued up the hill on foot. Her legs felt shaky and worry made her clumsy. Where was Lucifer now? She pushed her way past the brambles that swung out over the narrow track, tripping on tree roots, breathing in the smell of the wet undergrowth and mud. She reached another fork. Where now?

Listen for him.

It was as though she had Spirit's voice in her head, guiding her.

She paused. Taking a few deep breaths, she focused on feeling calm and still, then reached out with her mind, listening, waiting.

A feeling of sharp energy rolled towards her from the left. *Lucifer.* She didn't know how she knew he was there; she just did. She followed what her intuition told her and headed to the left.

The path wound round a corner. And then she stopped. The black horse was in front of her, head down, grazing, reins by his hooves. She'd found him!

She fought the urge to run forward and grab him. *Be still. Be calm*. Focusing completely on the horse, blocking out other thoughts, she spoke to him softly. 'Hey, fella. How are you doing? You've had a bit of an adventure, haven't you?'

The gelding lifted his head abruptly. He stared, muscles tense.

'It's OK,' Ellie murmured. 'I'm not going to hurt you.'

Lucifer continued to stare at her, his ears back. She could sense his desire to be left alone.

She eased off the pressure, taking a step back.

I want to help. I'll listen if you want to talk.

She felt as if he was pushing her away further.

She responded by taking another step back and saw the surprise in his eyes. His ears flickered as though he wondered if she was really responding to him.

Is this far enough?

She waited. For a long, long moment Lucifer watched her, and then all of a sudden he put his head down and started to graze again.

Well, at least he's not running away, Ellie thought. She decided to wait it out. Patience, not impatience, was needed now. She breathed in and out, imagining her breath running all the way down her spine and into the earth. She wanted to be as calm and open as she could be. Closing her eyes, she imagined gathering together all the love in her heart and sending it through the air to Lucifer. He lifted his head for a second, still chewing a mouthful of grass as he looked at her. She met his gaze calmly. *I'm here to listen if you want to talk*.

A picture entered her mind but it fleeted away before she could see it properly. All that she caught was the image of a young black colt, just a few days old, standing by the body of a mare, and she felt an immense sense of loss and confusion. She shut her eyes and a jumbled mix of images started to crowd through her brain: the colt, several years older, in a field, pressed against a barbed-wire fence, being attacked by a group of horses; the mare again, her body still on the ground; a man shouting, hitting . . .

Ellie let the pictures flow, not questioning or pushing, just accepting what Lucifer showed her. She began to see the pictures as if she was the colt, felt the kicks from the other horses coming from the side and in front, heard the sound of squealing in the air, the flattened ears and whites of the eyes, felt the bite of the barbed wire as it punctured her skin where she was pressed against it – felt the terror and confusion he had experienced . . .

Oh, you poor thing. She could feel the pain resounding through her own body, her heart pounding, the fear streaming through her. The pictures slowed. Ellie waited, sending out love and sympathy. The pictures came, slower now, starting from the beginning.

She saw Lucifer as a very young foal and saw his mother, lying dead on the ground. She felt his bewilderment at the loss, saw him searching for milk and finding nothing until a lady came along, kind and warm-eyed, who brought milk in a bucket. Ellie felt his happiness as he grazed in a field, happiness that increased when the woman came and handled him and chatted to him.

Ellie could tell there were no other horses around. Just the woman and the empty field. But Lucifer was happy. She saw him grow older and stronger and felt two winters pass, then she saw him in a horsebox being taken away.

She saw him arrive at a yard. There seemed to be horses everywhere. She felt the excitement running through him and saw him being turned out, not knowing what to do or how to act. Never having been with other horses, he instinctively behaved as he had when little, but the other horses met his playfulness with laid-back ears and annoyed squeals. The behaviour they would have put up with in a young foal was not acceptable in an almost fully grown young horse. She watched as he butted at them, prancing around, biting their necks. The other horses grew snappier. The tension built; there were bites and kicks, then suddenly he was being chased by a bay pony and several of the others. He was trapped by the fence. There were horses in front and the bay was kicking out, but the barbed-wire fence prevented him escaping. She felt the blows, the pain, the wire . . .

The pictures changed. He was in a stable being seen by a vet. They kept him in the stable for a while, but next time he was taken out to the field he didn't want to go, biting and kicking as he was led there, with the rough male groom smacking and shouting at him.

I'm scared. It hurts, she heard his thoughts, but the groom didn't. He was just concerned with forcing the horse to do what he wanted.

As soon as Lucifer was through the gate, she saw him standing, overwhelmed with fear. He galloped at any of the horses who came near, biting and kicking, terrified they would attack him again, and desperate to keep them away.

'Oh, Lucifer, you've been so frightened,' whispered Ellie.

He snorted and more pictures came. He was sold from the yard to a lady with no other horses. There she could see he had felt peace and contentment. Ellie saw him start going to shows. Enjoying it. She could sense from the happy feelings he sent to her that he liked being in the show ring, liked the praise and the judges who patted him, and the excitement of his owner when they won.

She risked a gentle question. *But what about the other horses in the ring?*

He sent her a picture of the other horses trotting round, all listening to their owners, ignoring the gelding. No horses attacked each other in the show ring. *It's safe there*, he replied.

And then you came here, to Uncle Len's?

Yes.

She saw how it must have appeared to the gelding. It must have seemed like the first yard he'd been taken to. No wonder he had tried to keep everyone away – the grooms, the other horses. Ellie remembered the bay pony kicking him in his memories and realized that the pony who had attacked him had looked similar to Merlin.

Her heart twisted. Any final remnants of bitterness towards him faded. She could understand what he'd been feeling, why he'd attacked the old pony, scared out of his wits as the old memories were stirred up when Merlin was put in the field with him.

Going up to him, Ellie put her arms gently round his neck, giving him all the love she could, wishing she could make him better and take the memories away.

She knew it was the same as with Spirit. The past could not be wiped out; bad memories could not simply be erased. She could give him relief by listening and loving, but she couldn't make him forget. However, she could help him.

I can do something, she told him. *I'll find a way*

to make sure you're not put out in the field with any other horses and maybe you can move round to the stables where Spirit is. You won't have to see the other horses all the time there. Only Spirit, and he would never hurt you.

He nuzzled her and she saw an image of Luke, overlaid with fear and confusion. *I was trying to please him. He just kept hitting me. I don't understand. I had to get away.*

A picture of Lucifer's last owner came into her mind. The lady's hands were feather light, her aids barely perceptible. Ellie felt Lucifer's willingness to please, to be as good as he could. Suddenly she got it. Deep down all he wanted to do was make his rider happy. He liked to be ridden lightly. The lighter the pressure, the better he would go.

I'll help you, she told him. *I promise.* Lucifer snorted and pushed his head against her chest.

'Come on,' she said softly. 'Let's go home.'

Chapter Fifteen

'So, you're saying I have to do almost nothing?' Luke stared at Ellie. 'You're mad. He'll be doing a bronco act in a second.'

'No, he won't.' Ellie patted Lucifer, feeling his anxiety as he regarded Luke. All the way back to the stables, she had been talking to him, telling him it would be OK. She hoped it had got through to him.

Spirit had been waiting where she'd left him and she had ridden Lucifer back, leading Spirit. She had sat as still as possible in the saddle, using only the gentlest aids, and he had behaved perfectly all the way home. But once they were near the yard she'd felt his tension build.

Luke had been on the drive. He had just returned on his motorbike. His face had been a picture of astonishment and relief as he looked at Ellie riding Lucifer.

'You've got him!'

'Yes, I found him up the mountain.'

'Thank God. Stu's gone out on Barney. I'll text to let him know you're back.' Luke pulled out his phone.

'OK, but then we're going back to the ring. I want you to ride him. I've had an idea of how to make him go better.' Ellie hoped that Lucifer trusted her enough now to let Luke ride him again. If she could just persuade Luke to ride him quietly, to ask instead of tell, and to use the smallest cues possible, then maybe Lucifer would start going well again in the ring.

At first Luke hadn't been that keen, but Ellie had insisted. 'Luke, you owe me one. I got him back here. I think I know how to get him going better.' She frowned. 'You said after I worked out what was wrong with Troy that you'd listen to me next time,' she reminded him. 'So listen.'

'OK then. I guess it's worth a try. After all, Len's way's sure as hell not working and we need to sort this out. If you think you know how to sort it, let's try.' Luke grinned. 'Bring on the horse-whispering!'

'This isn't horse-whispering!' Ellie said. 'I'll just be telling you how to ride him.'

Luke held up his hands. 'Whatever. I'm putty in your hands. Just tell me what to do and I'll do it. The worst that can happen is I get dumped on the ground again.'

Ellie felt a rush of warmth. Luke could be arrogant and irritating at times but you could certainly never accuse him of unwillingness to try new things. 'OK. Get on and ride him lightly then.'

'Yes, boss.' Luke put his foot in the stirrup. Ellie brought her thoughts away from Luke and focused completely on Lucifer, reading the signals he was giving with his body language, sending his emotions. She could feel tension in the air around him and she sent him all the reassurance she could. *It'll be OK.* Looking at Luke, long-legged in the saddle, she hoped she was right.

Luke started to shorten his reins. 'No,' she said quickly. 'Keep them long and when you use your legs barely squeeze. Do as little as you can.'

Luke nodded and didn't even squeeze; he clicked his tongue and the horse walked out into the school. 'Just walk him round on a loose rein to start,' Ellie instructed. 'I think he's been fighting you because you've been putting so much pressure on him.'

To her relief, Luke seemed prepared to stick to his agreement to try what she suggested. He rode very lightly, his hands barely touching the black gelding's mouth. Lucifer's tense walk relaxed and by the time he had walked all the way round the school his stride had started to lengthen and his neck arch over. Reaching the gate, he slowed.

'Let him stop if he wants,' Ellie said suddenly. 'Let's see what he wants to do.' Lucifer stopped and backed up obediently.

Not this time, she told him in her head, realizing her intuition had been right before. *It's not what Luke wants at the moment, but thank you for trying.*

Lucifer snorted and walked on calmly. The next time round he didn't stop. Ellie's heart swelled with hope. It was working. It was really working!

'Try him in a trot.'

Luke clicked his tongue and the gelding moved into a smooth, flowing trot. Luke gently guided him round circles and serpentines, changing the rein.

Ellie knew she could start to leave them to it. Climbing on to the gate, she watched as Luke and Lucifer worked together. When Luke tried cantering and came across the school, Lucifer thought they were changing direction and changed legs, but instead of telling him off Luke realized the horse was just attempting to do what was right. He simply slowed him down and asked him to canter again, then carried on the circle. The next time Lucifer didn't change legs, but carried on in a canter all the way round. With every minute that passed, Ellie could see the understanding between the pair of them growing. There were still moments of tension, but every time Luke felt one, he let the horse try what he wanted to do and then quietly rode on.

'Ellie!' Ellie jumped and looked round. It was Stuart. 'I just got back. I got Luke's text. What's happened? Where did you find Lucifer?' He stared at Luke and Lucifer incredulously. 'Look at him! Look how he's going!'

Ellie smiled happily. 'I found him up the mountain. Luckily, he was OK. When I was bringing him back I just had this idea that Luke had been riding him the wrong way. That he needed really light handling – the lighter, the better. He's been trying it out and it's working.'

'Well, if it carries on working your uncle's going to be a very happy man.' Stuart looked at her, a glint in his eye. 'What is it you do?'

Ellie frowned as she looked into the ex-jockey's face. 'What do you mean?'

'Well, first Picasso, then Troy, then this. Not to mention that horse of yours who you've rehabilitated.' Stuart folded his arms and looked at her curiously. 'What's the trick, Ellie?'

Ellie looked at Lucifer. 'There's no trick. I've just learned to listen.'

Stuart looked at her for a moment. 'Well, keep on listening. You're an asset to the yard.' He sucked the air in through his teeth and chuckled. 'I wonder what your uncle's going to say when he sees this.' With another chuckle, he walked off.

Ellie felt a glow inside. It was lovely to feel accepted by Stuart, lovely to feel that she was managing to help the horses and do some good.

Luke brought Lucifer back to a walk. Although

they were the far side of the school, Ellie saw his lips moving in praise as he patted the gelding. He rode over on a loose rein, looking totally nonplussed. 'You were right. If I ride him like you said he goes so much better. I'll make that do for now, though, he's had a tough morning.' He threw his leg over Lucifer's neck and dismounted.

Ellie went over to Lucifer and stroked his nose. *Thank you*, she told the gelding in her head. Her heart swelled with gratitude that he had been generous enough to let Luke try again. He nuzzled her.

'He looked like a different horse,' she said to Luke.

'He felt like a different one,' said Luke. 'Riding him lightly really worked. Nice one, Ellie.'

Lucifer nuzzled Ellie. 'We'll have to help him on the yard too. I think he needs to be in a quieter stable, maybe round by Spirit where he doesn't have to see the other horses all the time. Will you help me persuade Uncle Len?'

Luke nodded. 'Easy. I reckon when Len sees how well Lucifer's starting to go, he won't argue. Not that he'd stand a chance.' He grinned at her. 'You were seriously fierce with me earlier.'

'No, I wasn't!' Ellie protested.

'You so were. It's a good thing, though,' said Luke, opening the gate and leading Lucifer through. 'You're only like that because you care. You could stand back and do nothing – lots of people would – but you don't.' He looked at her. 'Not ever. That's cool.' Taken aback by the completely unexpected compliment, Ellie blushed.

Luke smiled. 'Look, the important thing is that Lucifer's not trying to kill me any more. If he carries on like this he might even win at the show. And before you say anything, Ellie Carrington,' he added quickly, raising his eyebrows at her, 'it's not *all* about winning for me.' Ellie's face was about to soften when Luke's eyes lit up with a wicked glint. 'After all, if he wins I might have a good chance with Anna Hallett!'

With an incorrigible chuckle, he led Lucifer down the slope.

Ellie shook her head. Honestly! She watched him leave, then giggled. Even though she sometimes accused him of arrogance, he had listened to her when she'd told him how to help Lucifer. He'd listened and done it without arguing. *Which is more than I did when Spirit was telling me what to do*, she realized guiltily. *Maybe I'm worse than Luke.*

Not any more, she decided. *From now on, I really will listen – in all ways.*

When Len returned from the show he was initially sceptical about the breakthrough in Lucifer's behaviour, but after Luke had brought the gelding out and shown him, Len was forced to admit they were right.

'Well, I'll be . . .' He trailed off, shaking his head as he watched Lucifer calmly responding to Luke's light cues. 'And it was you who thought of this?' he said, looking at Ellie.

She nodded without saying anything. She was glad for Lucifer's sake she had helped but not for her uncle's. She still hated him for putting Merlin down.

'Ellie thinks he's been scared in the past by other horses and we should put him in a quieter place on the yard, maybe round by Spirit,' Stuart said.

Len watched the gelding do a flying change and nodded. 'Fine by me. Whatever keeps him sweet.'

By the end of the day, Lucifer was bedded down in the stable next to Spirit. He was much calmer there without the constant coming and going.

Over the next two weeks, he stopped kicking at his door and tossing his head. He didn't seem to mind Spirit being nearby and it was clear he was developing a real affection for Ellie. Soon he was whinnying whenever she came round the corner. She made sure she talked to him every day, listening to what he'd been through and sending him love. Simply by listening to his memories, it seemed to make him feel happier.

Noticing the bond Lucifer was developing with her, Stuart put her in charge of grooming and feeding him. Luke took to riding him in the afternoons when

Ellie was back from school so she could watch and help. Lucifer got better and better. Ellie found herself really looking forward to the time she spent with Luke. They were both equally determined and focused, talking about Lucifer tirelessly, discussing how to give him the best chance in the ring.

Now they had Lucifer's trust, they knew they had to slowly start increasing the pressure put on him, in case the judge rode him strongly. They did it little by little, watching Lucifer's reactions carefully and responding by easing off the pressure whenever it was too much for him – being very horse-whispery as Ellie liked to tease Luke at every possible opportunity. And they saw an improvement every day. Len left them to it – he was no fool when it came to horses. Seeing how well they were doing, and being very busy with the other horses, he kept an eye on them but did not interfere.

Ellie wondered constantly how Lucifer would do at the show. She was taking Picasso in the show herself – but it was Lucifer who was filling her thoughts for the moment.

I hope he does well, she prayed as she groomed him the day before the show. She'd washed his tail and his coat was shining like polished ebony. Looking at him standing calmly while she brushed him over, she could hardly believe that just two weeks ago he had been so hostile.

'Don't you let me down with Anna Hallett tomorrow,' she sighed.

Anna had been supposed to ride him that week but she'd been too busy with exams. Ellie was feeling slightly worried about it. She hoped Anna would ride him lightly and give him the best chance. The judge would only ride him briefly but Anna would be on his back for a long time, and if she was too firm with him Ellie wasn't sure how he'd react.

Just then, Lucifer started slightly as Joe looked over the stable door.

'Hi there. I've done his tack – it's in the lorry. Do you want me to do Picasso's too?'

'Oh, yes please!' Ellie said, smiling at him. 'Thanks!'

Things were getting easier with Joe. Having Lucifer to focus her thoughts on had really helped. The pain she'd felt when she and Joe had decided to be just friends had begun to fade. She could laugh and chat with him now without feeling torn up inside. In fact, she even found herself occasionally wondering if they really had been that perfect for each other after all. She loved Joe to pieces but he did think and act differently from her in so many ways. She was glad they were still best friends, though. She knew he was still deeply upset about Merlin and didn't want to be avoiding him when he needed support. As he'd said, she was determined they'd always be close.

'I can't believe what a difference you've made to

Lucifer,' Joe said as he looked at the black gelding. 'There were Dad and Luke fighting with him and then suddenly, in one afternoon, you have this idea to treat him in a different way.' He shook his head. 'I still don't understand how you knew what he needed.'

Ellie smiled. 'Just instinct, I guess.'

Chapter Sixteen

The next morning, Ellie crawled out of bed at 4 a.m., helped load the horses and then climbed into the living accommodation of the horsebox. While Joe and Luke plugged themselves into their iPods, she promptly fell asleep on the sofa there until they arrived at the show at 5.30 a.m.

'Wakey wakey!' She became aware of something tickling her face and opened her eyes to see Luke grinning at her, tickling her face with a cactus cloth.

She groaned.

'Come on, Sleeping Beauty! We're here!'

'Here you go,' Joe said, handing her a mug of tea, while Luke threw open the jockey door and jumped out on to the show ground.

'Thanks.' Feeling crumpled, Ellie tightened her ponytail and went down the steps. The sun was just starting to rise in the sky, lightening the dark. Taking a deep breath of the fresh cool air, Ellie felt herself start to wake up. All around them were other lorries and people unloading horses and ponies.

'Time to get the horses out,' Joe told her as Len went off to check what was happening. Joe and Luke undid the ramp. As well as Lucifer, there were Picasso and Barney who would both be in the open working hunter pony classes, Wisp, who Joe would ride in the 153-centimetre show hunter pony class, and Gabriel, who Luke was taking in the Intermediate working hunter class. Spirit had come too, because Picasso was much happier travelling with Spirit in the horsebox.

Gabriel's class was the first of the working hunter pony classes. It started at 8 a.m. but Ellie didn't have time to see much of it because she was too busy exercising Picasso and getting him used to the show ground. The horses were usually worked in first thing, then prepared for their classes. Still, as she was working Picasso in, she caught sight of Luke doing his individual show for the judge. He pulled off a foot-perfect individual show with the fastest gallop of the class. He'd already gone clear in the jumping phase of the class and the judges placed him first. Luke came out grinning, the red rosette clipped on to the string of his number. Ellie and Joe rode to meet him. 'Nailed it!' he said, high-fiving Ellie.

'Well done!' she said in delight.

'Great start!' said Len, patting Gabriel's neck. 'Let's carry it on,' he said, looking at Ellie and Joe.

Barney was next in the ring. While Joe was competing, Luke brought Lucifer out and Ellie started preparing Picasso for the ring. His class was next. Luke had just started working Lucifer in when Anna and Jeff arrived. Anna was looking immaculate in a black jacket that showed off her slender waist, tight spotless cream breeches and shiny riding boots. Her dark hair was held back in a bun and the red stock around her neck was perfectly tied.

Ellie broke off from polishing Picasso. 'Anna, can I talk to you for a minute?'

Anna was busy watching Luke, who had halted close by and was now practising reining back. She gave Ellie an irritated look. 'What?'

'I need to tell you about riding Lucifer.'

Anna frowned. 'I hardly think I need advice from you.' It was clear she thought of Ellie as much younger.

Ellie refused to be put off. 'Lucifer can be difficult.'

'He doesn't look difficult to me,' said Anna as Lucifer backed five paces, halted and walked forward again obediently.

'I know. But he is. You have to ride him gently,' Ellie felt her anxiety growing. How could she make Anna understand? 'Really gently.' She looked at Lucifer and caught Luke's eye. She knew he was listening.

'Right. Thanks,' Anna said dismissively.

'I mean it. Please, just use the lightest possible aids and –'

'Hi,' Anna cut her off as she went over to Luke. 'He's looking good.'

Luke smiled at her. 'So are you.'

Anna blushed.

Luke dismounted. 'He should have a really good chance in the ring, but there are some things you need to know about riding him if you want the best out of him.'

'Sure, what do I have to do?' Anna looked up eagerly at Luke.

'Ride him gently, very gently, use very light aids,' Luke echoed Ellie's words.

'OK, right.' Anna nodded, agreeing with every word he said. 'Of course I will.'

Ellie felt her mouth drop open. Luke put his hand on Anna's back. 'Maybe you should get on and I'll give you a quick lesson on how to make him go best,' he said smoothly.

'Sure thing.' Anna smiled and mounted. She walked Lucifer away.

Luke shot a look at Ellie and grinned.

Luke's charms worked on Anna and she rode Lucifer on the lightest possible contact. Ellie didn't have time to watch for long, though, because she was due in the ring herself. Barney had won his class too and Len was delighted. To Ellie's disappointment, she didn't quite manage to make it three in a row. Picasso jumped a clear round and did a really good show, but the judge placed him fourth. Ellie would have liked to win but she felt OK about the fourth place. She knew Picasso had gone really well, but at the end of the day it came down to the judge's opinion.

She wondered what her uncle would say, but as she rode over to him he just nodded philosophically. 'Next time,' he told her. 'You rode well.'

Ellie took Picasso back to the box. She rubbed him down and put him back in the lorry with Spirit, then went see what was happening with Lucifer.

He was just going into the ring. He looked wonderful. Luke had groomed him to perfection and as he trotted round, his hooves skimming smoothly across the short grass, his neck arched, his black coat gleaming, he caught the eye in a way none of the other horses did. After all the horses had been ridden round together, Lucifer was pulled in top of the line. It seemed to take forever for the judging of the individual show and the confirmation, but eventually it was over and the two smartly dressed judges began to confer, as the horses walked on round the ring.

'Oh, please, please, please let it be him!' Ellie prayed aloud.

'It will be,' Luke said, but he gripped Ellie's arm. The two of them were watching a little way away from Len and Jeff, while Joe was back at the box readying Wisp for his class. Ellie glanced at Luke's face and saw the tension in his jaw. 'Come on, come on,' he muttered as the steward started walking in Lucifer's direction. Ellie held her breath. Would Lucifer be called in first or would the steward go to the next horse along?

The steward pointed at Lucifer and called out Anna's number.

'They've won!' Luke exclaimed, grabbing Ellie in a bear hug and swinging her round. She squealed in surprise.

He put her down, laughing, his eyes sparkling with triumph. For a moment all she could think was how blue they were. 'He's got his ticket to Hickstead. First time out.'

Still in his arms and feeling rather breathless, Ellie grinned. 'We did it! We actually did it!'

As he looked down at her a strange expression passed across his face.

'What?' she demanded. He didn't say anything and she began to feel rather self-conscious, wondering if she had a smudge on her face or something. She tried to step back but his arms tightened round her.

'Do you ever wonder, Ellie,' he said suddenly. 'You and me?'

'You and me?' Ellie echoed in confusion. Her eyes widened as she realized what he meant. 'You and ME!' she spluttered. 'No!' She pulled away from him, shaking her head. 'Oh no, no, no, no, no!'

He grinned. 'I'll take that as a no then.'

Suspicion hit her. This had to be just one of his wind-ups. 'You're joking, aren't you? You're not serious?'

He just looked at her in reply, amusement glinting in his eyes.

Jeff and Len came walking over in their direction. Ellie went to meet them, her heart banging against her ribcage. Luke had just been joking, hadn't he? She glanced back at him. He gave her a broad grin. *Of course he was*, she told herself. *He's got enough on his plate with Sasha and Anna. As if he'd be interested in me as well.*

Jeff and Len were both delighted with Lucifer. 'What a win!' Jeff said. 'You've worked a miracle with that horse, Len, he's a different creature from the one I saw a few weeks ago.'

Ellie thought her uncle would take all the credit himself, but to her surprise he said, 'It's been a team effort. Everyone's been involved – Luke and Ellie most of all.'

Seeing her uncle's delight with the win, Ellie felt torn. She would never forgive him, but she was glad Lucifer had won. Anna was over the moon when she came out of the ring, and they headed back to the horsebox to tell Joe and have some champagne before Lucifer went into the hack championship.

Jeff handed the glasses out when they arrived.

'Here's to the whole of the High Peak Stables team!' he said as he poured out the bubbles.

They clinked their glasses together. Ellie took a gulp.

'One show, one win, can't ask for more than that,' said Jeff with satisfaction. He and Len started talking.

'We've still got our bet to go,' Ellie heard Anna say to Luke. The dark-haired girl was standing very close to him, her fingers playing with the stem of her wine glass. 'Who's going to get the HOYS ticket first then? You or me?' She looked up at him through her eyelashes.

'What I want to know is what does the winner get?' said Luke lazily.

Anna whispered something to him. He smiled and, moving her hair from her ear, murmured something back that made her blush. Ellie felt a stab of indefinable emotion and looked quickly away.

He's still going out with Sasha, she thought hotly. *He shouldn't be flirting like that with Anna!* And what about Uncle Len? He had already warned Luke off. Ellie felt a prickle of foreboding.

Suddenly very keen to escape from them, she joined Joe who was standing a little way off.

'Hi there. You OK?' he said.

'Yeah.'

'It's brilliant Lucifer won the class and it wouldn't

have happened without you working out how to ride him. Well done!'

'Thanks.'

They smiled at each other.

'I'd better finish preparing Wisp.'

'I'll give you a hand.'

Ellie followed Joe over to the pony. She could hear Jeff and Len talking loudly about Lucifer and what he would win that season. It seemed as if the threat of losing the Equi-Glow sponsorship was well and truly over.

She silently thanked Spirit. No one would ever know the part he had played in it all. Without him, she wouldn't have found out what was wrong with Lucifer and Lucifer wouldn't have won.

Ellie sighed happily. Things were going well. Lucifer was content; she and Joe were back to being friends, and Luke . . . for a second she pictured his laughing blue eyes but she pushed them away . . . well, it had been lots of fun working with him and Lucifer.

Her life at High Peak Stables might be very different from her old life in New Zealand, but it was beginning to feel like *her* life and not just a life she had been dumped in and didn't belong to. She knew she would never stop missing her mum and dad but she also knew she couldn't cling to the past, hoping it would come back. It wouldn't. One of the many things Spirit had taught her in the last few months was that life moved on and you had to live in the present. Things were always changing and you had to change with them. You couldn't live in the past. Horses knew that.

'Earth to Ellie!' Joe pushed a bottle of hoof varnish into her hands. 'Of course, I could get Wisp ready all by myself at the ringside but you *did* offer, and standing there really isn't going to do the business.'

'Sorry!'

Live in the present, Ellie told herself with a smile. And, crouching down, she began to paint Wisp's hooves.

Night-time . . .

Later that night, when all the horses and tack had been unloaded from the lorry, Ellie went to Spirit's stable. He was lying down now, his legs tucked under him, his muzzle resting on the straw. He whickered as she opened the door.

The stable was warm and sweet-smelling and the straw rustled under her feet as she went over to him. She sat down, curling up in the space between his front and back legs. Putting her arm round his back, she felt the tension, adrenaline and excitement of the day slowly fade away and sighed. It had been a great show – Lucifer had also gone on to win the hack championship, and then Gabriel had won the working hunter pony championship, with Barney being made the Reserve Champion. However, she was glad it was all over now. Of all the places in the world, this was where she most wanted to be.

Leaning against Spirit's warm shoulder, she gently traced the lines of his face. She'd always known she was lucky to have him, but only that day had she begun to realize quite how special he was. Looking back, she could see how much he had taught her in the last few months, both through talking to her and showing her through his own behaviour. He hadn't just taught her how to speak to horses; he had also shown her the importance of listening to her instincts, being patient, letting go, moving on. It was as though, day after day, he had taken it on himself to guide her, gently nudging her along.

Ellie knew that many people would say she was mad. Her uncle, for one. She could just imagine his scornful laugh if she said Spirit had been setting out to teach her things. But she was sure he had.

'You're amazing,' she whispered, kissing him. After all he had been through in his own past, Spirit could have hated people, but when he had met her he had been prepared to trust and love again. Horses were incredible – Spirit most of all.

Ellie started thinking about all they could do together, the horses they could help. She wanted to use what he had taught her, make as big a difference as she could. She wondered about the horses she would talk to next. Who would they be? What would be the matter with them? What stories would they tell?

Spirit nuzzled her, bringing her back to the present. His wise eyes met hers and she smiled. Whatever was in the future, one thing was for sure: they would love each other, truly and completely. Most things changed in life, but she knew that never would.

Not ever, she told him fiercely.

Resting her head against his neck, she let the rest of the world fade away. It was just her and Spirit. Outside a barn owl hooted in the dark, wide night as the shadows slowly deepened around them.

Now Ellie's found him, she'll never let go . . .

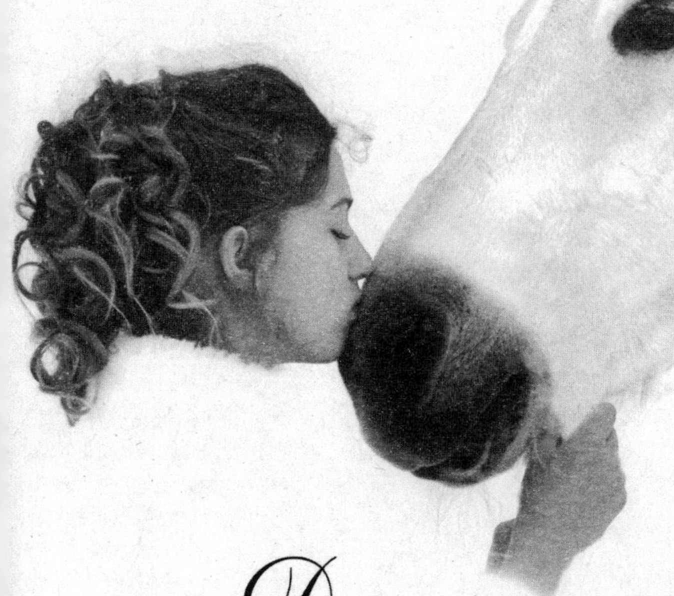

Discover each of the books in this stunning

Loving Spirit

quartet.

It all started with a Scarecrow.

Puffin is seventy years old.

Sounds ancient, doesn't it? But Puffin has never been so lively. We're always on the lookout for the next big idea, which is how it began all those years ago.

Penguin Books was a big idea from the mind of a man called Allen Lane, who in 1935 invented the quality paperback and changed the world. **And from great Penguins, great Puffins grew, changing the face of children's books forever.**

The first four Puffin Picture Books were hatched in 1940 and the first Puffin story book featured a man with broomstick arms called Worzel Gummidge. In 1967 Kaye Webb, Puffin Editor, started the Puffin Club, promising to **'make children into readers'**. She kept that promise and over 200,000 children became devoted Puffineers through their quarterly instalments of *Puffin Post*, which is now back for a new generation.

Many years from now, we hope you'll look back and remember Puffin with a smile. **No matter what your age or what you're into, there's a Puffin for everyone.** The possibilities are endless, but one thing is for sure: whether it's a picture book or a paperback, a sticker book or a hardback, **if it's got that little Puffin on it – it's bound to be good.**